Boys No More

True Stories of WWII

ANNETTE OPPENLANDER

First published by Annette Oppenlander, 2020
First Edition
annetteoppenlander.com
Averesch 93, 48683 Ahaus
Text Copyright: Annette Oppenlander 2020
ISBN: 978-3-948100-20-9 eBook
ISBN: 978-3-948100-21-6 Paperback

Editing: Yellow Bird Editors
Design: fiverr.com/akira007

DEDICATION

For my father,
who shared his stories with me,
so I could share them with the world,
to not be forgotten.

ALSO BY ANNETTE OPPENLANDER

A Different Truth *(Historical Mystery – Vietnam War Era)*
Escape from the Past: The Duke's Wrath I *(Time-travel Adventure Trilogy)*
Escape from the Past: The Kid II
Escape from the Past: At Witches' End III
Surviving the Fatherland: A True Coming-of-age Love Story Set in WWII
(Historical Biographical Fiction)
Everything We Lose: A Civil War Novel of Hope, Courage and Redemption
Where the Night Never Ends: A Prohibition Era Novel
When They Made Us Leave *(WWII)*
A Lightness in My Soul *(Biographical - WWII)*
The Scent of a Storm *(WWII and German Reunification)*
So Close to Heaven *(Biographical - Napoleon Wars)*
When the Skies Rained Freedom *(Berlin Airlift)*

German Novels
Vaterland, wo bist Du? Roman nach einer wahren Geschichte
(biografisch – 2. Weltkrieg/Nachkriegszeit)
Erzwungene Wege: Historischer Roman *(2. Weltkrieg)*
47 Tage: Wie zwei Jungen Hitlers letztem Befehl trotzten
(Novelle)
Immer der Fremdling: Die Rache des Grafen *(Gaming Zeitreise Mittelalter)*
Als Deutschlands Jungen ihre Jugend verloren *(2. Weltkrieg – Sammlung)*
Bis uns nichts mehr bleibt *(amerikanischer Bürgerkrieg)*
Ewig währt der Sturm *(2. Weltkrieg – Flucht und Vertreibung)*
Leicht wie meine Seele *(2. Weltkrieg – Novelle)*
Endlos ist die Nacht *(amerikanische Prohibition)*
Das Kreuz des Himmels *(biografisch – Napoleon Kriege)*

ACKNOWLEDGMENTS

I don't want an intellectual education. Knowledge ruins our youth." –Adolf Hitler

"If we have power, we'll never give it up again unless we're carried out of our offices as corpses." –Propaganda Minister Joseph Goebbels

"For out of black soul's night have stirred dawn's cold gleam,
morning's singing bird. Let black day die, let black flag fall, let raven call,
let new day dawn of black reborn."
–George Woodcock from "Black Flag" in Collected Poems (1983)

INTRODUCTION

In 2002 I began interviewing my parents who experienced WWII as children and youths in Germany. Initially, I wanted to capture their memories and preserve them for our family. I wanted to understand what had happened to the civilian children of that time who were born at the wrong time and place, when insanity ruled and nothing was safe. I also wanted to provide a glimpse behind the scenes of civilian Germany against the backdrop of the country's physical, sociological and emotional annihilation during and after WWII—an era silenced or ignored as the last of the surviving war children die off seventy-five plus years later.

Even though the following stories take place during and shortly after WWII, they are not typical war stories. They don't feature battles, soldiers and crazy German generals. These stories describe what happened to the teen boys who got caught up in this time, 9th and 10th graders who should've been attending school. They truly were born at the wrong time in the wrong place.

All stories in this collection are true. But what does that really mean? Historical fiction is tricky business as it requires authors to reimagine what is no longer. To do this in the most authentic way possible, authors spend a lot of time studying historical events. Part of this study includes interviews, videos, history books, letters, diaries and newspapers.

The stories of this collection are chronologically ordered, starting in February 1945. In *Visit of Consequence,* my father, Günter, and his best friend, Helmut, had the glorious idea of visiting Günter's brother Hans at a military camp near Düsseldorf. Problem was, to see Hans they had to cross the Rhine, which proved to be a fateful mistake.

In the novelette, *47 Days*, just two months before Germany capitulated, Hitler called to arms all boys born 1928 and 1929. In early March 1945 Günter and Helmut were mustered and drafted to defend the fatherland—though everyone knew that the war was lost. After all, Germany's soldiers were returning defeated, their uniforms torn and their guns and bellies empty. But to revolt and not follow military orders of the SS meant certain death. And so Günter and Helmut decided to hide and not report to the city of Marburg, two-hundred kilometers from home. For nearly seven weeks they crisscrossed the hilly land near their home, always on guard, always afraid. Being caught meant certain execution.

A Lightness in My Soul is based on the experience of Arthur, a German boy who was slightly younger and had just spent two years in a Bavarian youth camp when American troops appeared. It was April 30, 1945. Those boys in their naivety had been told that Hitler was winning. They had been sheltered, playing war games with sticks and trying to remain on the right side of their fanatical teacher, Herr Braun. When those American soldiers marched into school,

Arthur and his classmates were incredulous. What followed is a story that few know about, because Arthur never breathed a word. For seventy-five years he kept his ordeal locked up deep inside. To let it out was so disturbing and so painful, he was afraid sharing his story would cause his mind to break.

The last story, *An Unexpected Return*, is also true. When Hans, Günter's older brother returned home from a British POW camp, he was only a shell of himself. He'd been gone less than a year and yet, the experience of war and prison changed him forever. Turning eighteen, he entered adulthood as an old man.

PROLOGUE

What made me do act this way? Even now, more than seventy years later, I cannot say. Not exactly, at least.

Oh, I do have an inkling. So let me explain.

I was the middle of three boys, my brother, Hans, just about a year older, my younger brother, Siegfried, eight years my junior. In our German home my father ruled and we obeyed, his box to the ear quicker than the strike of a cobra. Yet, we knew our place, each of us bonded within to our family, with homemade sweetbread, butter and red current jam on Sunday mornings, and the conviction that life would always continue as it had.

That is until the war started and my father went away. From then on, as months turned to years and life grew into the monstrous chore of survival, I forgot my good German manners, my obedience. I became someone else, a person I sometimes didn't recognize, a being that fought and scraped like the lowest animal—or did stupid stuff because it no longer mattered.

Until that fateful spring in 1945, I never realized what 'home' meant and what I'd do to keep it in my heart. How deep Hitler's evil reached. How it changed the way I looked at the world and forced me to make an impossible choice.

Anymore, my memory plays tricks. But though I struggle to keep my day-to-day life straight, I clearly remember the day everything started.

I remember when we were ordered to die for the Fatherland.

VISIT OF CONSEQUENCE

Solingen, Germany, October 1944

I lay on my bed watching my brother pack. Hans's face was stoic. He moved faster than usual, but his arms and legs kept bumping into things. Picture frames and clothes tumbled to the floor, and he forgot to pick them up.

I looked around the room we'd shared for as long as I could remember. How I had wanted a place to myself. Now I just wanted my brother. I'd share the room until I was an old man rather than see Hans go off like this.

"Can't you say you're sick?" I pleaded.

Hans stuffed socks into a canvas bag. "When they say you're drafted, there's no arguing."

I stared at him, wanting to say more. Why didn't he yell or complain or kick something? I could have dealt with any of it—anything but the outward calm, the acceptance of fate. Instead I just asked, "You think you'll see Father?"

"Unlikely."

"You could ask." What I really wanted to know was if Hans was scared and to remind him to be careful. In the stuffiness of our room, the words refused to come. The feeling of helplessness was paralyzing, and I knew my words meant nothing. They were a mere scratch on a mountain.

I wrapped my arms around my knees and closed my eyes. It wouldn't be the last time I wished to jump out of my skin.

In the kitchen, Mother paced back and forth. "You're only seventeen," she wailed as she put out Hans's last breakfast, two slices of cornbread and blackberry jam we'd saved from last summer. "First your father, now you. What are we going to do? They're going to kill us all."

Hans took Mother's hand. "I'll be fine."

Watching my brother, something icy curdled my stomach. Each day The *Tageblatt* was filled with pages of obituaries, and Mother poured over them, searching for familiar names. My father had been transferred to the Eastern Front in the Balkans. He'd written once, but we'd heard nothing in months. His care packages were a distant memory.

For the rest of the meal we sat in silence, my brother's eyes shiny. Tears pressed against my skull, begging to come out.

Hans punched my arm as we headed for the door. "Stop acting like a stupid girl," he said, producing a watery grin. "Don't worry, you'll be next."

I cringed. Was that supposed to make me feel better? I felt torn between shouting an insult and hiding Hans in the attic.

We hugged and I watched my brother, trying to memorize his features. What did you say to somebody facing death? No words were right, so I said nothing.

As he took his leave, Hans's eyes, shiny with grief and longing, burned themselves into my memory like a scar.

"Just us now." Mother wiped her face.

I scanned the deserted kitchen table, my little brother watching us. At eight, he still didn't know what was going on. It was a good thing.

"I'll take care of you," I said, clearing my throat. "I'm going out to look for food." In truth, I needed time away from the apartment where everything reminded me that my family was shrinking. My father had left four years ago. I'd gotten used to that. At least I didn't always look at his empty seat now. But with Hans, it was as if a new hole had appeared in my life.

It was easier to be outdoors—to keep myself busy. Then I wouldn't think about how much I'd relied on my brother for support. Not the physical kind, but an emotional bond that had given me strength. In the absence of our father, we'd stuck together. Entering my room, I stared at the vacant bed, shadows filling its emptiness.

At that moment, I decided to stop reading the paper and listening to the radio. It was maddening to hear nothing but propaganda and listen to speeches about how we were supposed to fight for honor until the end. What did that mean anyway? All I cared about was getting Father and Hans home and food into my stomach. The only good thing was that I'd escaped the drills of the Hitler youth because I played accordion. Helmut hated every minute of it. As part of the youth band we visited hospitals and nursing homes, appeared at dances and festivals. The music allowed me to escape, if only for the time I played.

In early November Hans wrote and sent photos. He'd finished training and was waiting for marching orders. He looked strange in the uniform and fancy cap—older and somehow detached.

In his first letter after Christmas, Hans mentioned that he was stationed at an old farm near Neuss, Düsseldorf. "If you want to visit, I can arrange it." He wrote in his letter. I looked at Mother who was measuring cornmeal for bread.

It was the same every day. Cornmeal with water, no salt, no butter, no eggs.

"What does he mean?" I asked.

"He's missing us. How could he not?" Mother's voice wasn't quite steady, so I looked up. She was staring at the window and by the way her shoulders trembled, I thought she was crying. But when she turned her head, her eyes were dry.

"Damn war," she said quietly. Mother never swore, so this was more worrisome than her tears. "First, they send your father, now Hans. Who knows how long he'll be gone? Where they'll send him?" She sank onto the bench, the spot she always sat, and patted the stack of letters—first the tall pile—Father's letters—then Hans's little stack. "It's been more than five years already. How much longer…"

She closed her eyes. My hand found hers. It still rested on top of the piles as if she could conjure a connection with Father and Hans. "Maybe I can visit Hans. It's not that far, maybe sixty kilometers…three or four hours tops."

"If you get through."

"Of course, I'll get through. Helmut will go with me." I forced a smile. "Who knows, we may find something good to eat on the way." I let go of Mother's hand and abruptly rose. I didn't want to show her how I dreaded being on the road hungry. It was bad enough to roam around home, but riding our bikes for hours meant, we'd need decent supplies or be utterly miserable. And there was the other thing. Rumors had been growing that Allied troops were crossing France west toward us. It was a matter of time…

"…ful." Mother's dark eyes were on me.

"What?"

"I said, make sure you're careful."

I grinned. "Always."

It was February 22nd before we headed out because Helmut had waited to help his mother prep the garden for spring. While he lived in a tiny crooked half-timber house in Unnersberg, they had a vegetable patch that was protected by a fence. I on the other hand lived in a multi-family apartment, actually, there was an entire row of them. We had space behind our houses too, but it was impossible to protect anything edible from thieves.

That's how it is when you take everything away from the people. You send the shop owners to war, close bakeries and butchers, focus every shred of energy on manufacturing weapons, make them starve—survival is a strong instinct, so strong, people become thieves, stealing from their friends and neighbors. You lost your morals and your understanding of right and wrong.

We left after school. Though it was early afternoon, mist rose from the ground, white clouds drifted across fields and paths, dampness crept beneath our jackets and wet our skin. Still, I relished the freedom of movement, feeling my legs pump the pedals, the wind against my cheeks.

Each of us carried a few slices of cornbread, a bit of jam and two potatoes, courtesy of Helmut's mother.

As we reached the southern end of Düsseldorf, bomb craters appeared left and right, debris peppered the roads. Clean-up commandoes, mostly women, were moving, sorting and stacking bricks, concrete and wood. Along the Rhine River the city had been flattened, a nightmare of ruins and rubble. Dirty-faced children roamed, lugging raggedy bags, old pillowcases and battered suitcases to carry their finds. It was an ocean of rocks, dust and burned remains, the air sharp from the ashes of hundreds of fires. Of what, I wasn't so sure, didn't want to know, didn't want to look.

"Just like home," Helmut said, when we stopped to pee.

It was true. Four months ago, Solingen had suffered its worst bombing. Thousands of air mines, carpet and phosphor rained down, annihilating the town. It had been a weekend, I'd just been in the tub, when hell broke loose. The city had burned for a week.

"Let's cross," I said, eying the southern bridge, spanning across the Rhine. "How about we'll eat over there?" I pointed across the water where a meadow stretched for miles.

Squinting at the destruction, Helmut wordlessly mounted his bike.

On the left side of the Rhine we unpacked our lunch. The river flowed slowly...indifferently, a huge expanse of water more than a hundred yards wide. I carefully took a bit of the cornbread that resembled a collection of crumbles, made worse by the rough ride. I'd learned to eat slowly, drink water in-between, just to feel like my stomach was filling somewhat. Helmut was doing the same, staring gloomily at the water.

"You think they've got food for us?" he asked after a while.

"Hope so, surely Hans can organize something."

Again, silence settled. It wasn't uncomfortable, Helmut and I had been together since first grade—there was just nothing to say.

"You think they'll draft us too?" he asked as we packed up. Picnicking in February wasn't a good idea. It wasn't exactly wet, but the ground sent frozen darts up my back.

"Hans is in the signal corps. Maybe we'll join him."

"But we're only sixteen." Helmut's gaze wandered toward the river. Even from fifty some yards away, the Rhine's steady gurgling was noticeable. The sound calmed me, emitted a bit of steadiness I craved.

"Let's go, can't be far now."

After a few stops asking around, we approached the village of Schiefbahn. Had I not known there was a war on, I would've thought I was in a different country. Around us stretched fields planted with kale and leeks, farms dotted the landscape.

After we asked an old woman for the location of the *Wehrmacht*, she pointed down a narrow lane toward a large farm with a red-bricked farmhouse and matching stalls.

"Over there, look," Helmut cried.

Half covered by hawthorn and holly bushes, tents lined up next to an assembly of cars and two tanks. A squarish truck with a huge antenna parked to the side. Two men in uniform sat around a radio-like contraption, one of them wearing headphones.

"Can I help you?" A boy in uniform and not much older than Hans, eyed us suspiciously.

"I'm here to see my brother," I blurted. "Hans Schmidt, you know him?"

Unsmiling the boy produced a "Wait here," and disappeared.

"Looks like we're in the right place," Helmut whispered.

Faint stomping and snorts drifted across from the stalls. My brain immediately registered that there were live animals, a rarity these days. During our cross-country excursions, searching for food, we never saw any farm animals. They'd long been hidden away, killed for food—or stolen. My mouth watered. Animals meant roasts and sausages, butter, cream and milk.

"Günter." Hans rushed up to me grinning. "You made it."

I stared at my brother who'd left last fall, yet, seemed so much older. We hugged, something we'd rarely done before. Now it seemed to be the right thing.

"You look good," I managed. It was true. Hans looked much better fed than us, his uniform clean and orderly. He was shorter than I, but right now, he seemed six feet tall.

"We better get you situated," he said, shaking Helmut's hand. "You can sleep in the barn."

As Hans led the way to a two-story building behind the main house, I curiously watched the men surrounding the radio. Now a couple of them wore headphones, scribbling frantically.

"What are they doing?" I asked.

"Taking notes." Hans gave me a quick squeeze. "Can't tell you, brother. Military secrets." He pointed at the loft. "Up there. I'll get you blankets. Now I must report back."

Wait, I wanted to say. *Tell me what you're doing, how you feel in this strange world.* I wasn't used to my brother being so efficient, so grown up.

"He sure seems different," Helmut said. When I didn't answer, he continued, "Maybe we should walk around."

"I wouldn't do that." The voice belonged to a boy, who was maybe twelve or thirteen, carrying two blankets. "They like to be left alone." He grinned, a careless grin, I wasn't used to either. "I'm Tomas, Tom, this is our farm."

We introduced ourselves, and I marveled at the well-nourished boy. He'd likely neither starved nor seen any bombs drop from the sky.

Like it should be, the voice in my head commented. *Quit being an idiot.*

"How about I'll show you around?" Tom said. He gave us a strange look. "Maybe we'll find some grub first."

Fifteen minutes later we sat on the rim of a water basin inside the cowbarn, chewing a huge sandwich with butter and salami. I hadn't eaten cold cuts in four years, so the flavor hit my brain like a freight train. Salty, fatty, meaty...incredible. Helmut looked similarly engrossed, he hardly lifted his gaze from the bread. This was the real thing, sourdough rye, the roundish loaf a foot-and-a-half across.

It should've bothered us to sit in here, surrounded by manure and animal farts, but it didn't matter. Nothing mattered, but the food sliding through my throat, the feeling of growing fullness.

"Here you are." Hans marched toward us, even his steps seemed different—large and square and efficient. "I've got a bit of time now, told the Sergeant that you arrived."

"How long will you stay?" Tom asked.

I looked at Helmut and back at Tom and my brother, as my mind strayed to focus on the excellent food I'd just enjoyed. "No idea." But Monday morning I had to be back in school and Helmut at work. "Maybe till Sunday."

"I'll make sure that's all right," Hans said.

The rest of the afternoon, we climbed around the barn, tried out a rusty Deutz tractor and watched the animals. Tom's family also kept a half-dozen pigs, four geese, a flock of chickens with a huge mean-looking rooster. All livestock was indoors and that had nothing to do with the weather.

"It's so peaceful here," Helmut said while we washed up for dinner. "Doesn't even feel like there's a war on."

I threw a glance at the men who crowded near the radio contraption. Now there were four of them, all wearing headphones—one of them with the insignia of a sergeant— Hans's boss. Hans had left a while ago and I thought I recognized him inside the radio truck with the huge antenna.

We ate dinner in the farmer's huge kitchen, ten of us— two sets remained empty—because as Hans said, military business never stopped. Who cared? I was too busy stuffing myself with fried potatoes, bratwurst, mountains of kale with onions, followed by vanilla pudding with canned cherries.

Only when I finished did I realize that Tom still had his father at the table. Again, envy reared its ugly head. Tom's father had a ruddy face from a life spent outdoors and humungous salt and pepper eyebrows that matched his hair. He didn't say much, didn't smile and when he got up from the table, I noticed that he had a serious limp, lifting his entire leg to take a step.

"Lost his leg in a tractor accident," Tom said quietly. I chewed my lip—so much for being envious.

Immediately after dinner, Hans and the other radiomen excused themselves. Hans cuffed me in the shoulder. "See you in the morning."

Lying in my haybed, my last thoughts were on my brother and the question, why he had appeared so serious during dinner. All of them had, but then, maybe that was the way they always acted.

"Up, quick!" A disembodied voice urged. "Meet me at the truck." In the low light of an oil lamp, Hans stood fully dressed in uniform.

My brain scrambled to form words. "What? Now?"

"Yes, immediately." What shook me awake weren't Hans's words, but the way he sounded. Scared. Nervous. "I'll leave you the lamp."

Helmut sat up, hay stalks in his hair. "What happened?"

Instead of answering, Hans hurried down the ladder. I scrambled to my feet, pulling on clothes and shoes.

Outside, in the light of two lanterns, I noticed the grass was bare. Tents and equipment had been packed, two tanks and two vehicles were missing.

"What's going on?" I asked, but Hans just gripped my arm.

"No time, get your bikes, we're leaving."

That's when I heard it: long whistling and shrieking, a

pause, and then…detonations. I'd never heard it, but immediately realized that this was artillery fire. It sounded different from air bombs. Either way, the Allies were on the move west, the rumors true. Adrenalin surged through me in a wave, my insides grew hot. It wasn't exactly fear, rather a general fury at the unseen enemy…and my helplessness.

Damn war!

I motioned Helmut to follow me. The sergeant was already sitting in the driver's seat of the radio truck and when Hans threw our bikes in the back, we wordlessly jumped in after them.

Slowly, much too slowly we returned to the main road toward the south bridge in Neuss. Had it only been yesterday afternoon since we rode the other way?

"Americans are coming," Hans said. They'll want to take the bridge.

"Where are we going?" I asked. But Hans didn't hear because in that moment, a huge explosion rattled our truck. We lurched forward into the darkness. Along the way I noticed the faint outlines of people rushing the same way. They carried suitcases, pushed strollers and dragged carts. How they could be so quick to pack, I didn't know. Fact was, they meant to be gone when the Americans arrived.

The closer we got to the bridge, the more crowded the road became. No longer could we drive through the middle, we rolled along, no quicker than the slowest grandfather.

Then we stopped.

"Why aren't we moving?" Helmut asked. I could tell by his quivering voice that he was scared.

"Too many people heading across the bridge," a radioman in the passenger seat shouted.

"Damn." That came from the sergeant.

"If they get close enough, they'll arrest us," Hans said. He'd moved closer to me, our shoulders touching. "We're going across, back to our old camp."

I looked at the wall of technology, buttons and levers, headphones and cables. How could Hans make sense of this? In my mind's eye I saw Americans waving machine guns at us, taking aim. What would stop them from shooting us dead?

Minutes ticked by while the throng of people around us thickened. Soon, they stood so close, I saw their faces in the headlight of the following car. They appeared ghostly, their eyes wide with fear, their fingers clamped around their cases or the hands of children.

Sweat seeped from my armpits, then my forehead. I wiped across with a sleeve, watching, waiting. We were inside a military truck. For the Allies, we were soldiers—the enemy. Another image formed. Mother at home, clutching two letters to her chest. Death announcements of her two oldest sons.

"Enough," the sergeant shouted upfront. He ripped open the door, causing a woman close to the truck to stumble. Ignoring her, he pushed his way through the crowd and disappeared.

"Maybe we should take our bikes and try it alone," Helmut said.

"If the Allies get close, you won't make it," Hans said.

"If we stay here for hours, we won't either," I said as another wave of heat surged up my neck. "Stupid war."

Hans's hand landed on my sleeve. "Patience. A few minutes won't hurt." In that moment I was immensely thankful for my brother's calm voice. When had he become so mature?

A particularly loud explosion rattled the truck's windows. Outside, hysterical shouts rose. The crowd grew denser, if that was possible.

Whistles trilled and then the sergeant crawled back

inside. "We'll get priority. Won't be long now."

Sure enough the front of the crowd somehow parted and foot by foot we crept toward the bridge. Near the onramp, soldiers had cordoned off the throng. As we slowly crossed the Rhine and the noise of the approaching artillery quieted, I leaned back and closed my eyes. Nobody spoke. Relief and worry mingled: I was glad to get away, but how far could we flee? If the Allies crossed the bridge, they would surely reach Solingen.

It was only a matter of time.

Next to me Hans had his eyes closed. Was he thinking the same? He wore the German uniform, carried a target on his back. I wanted to talk to him but didn't want the others to hear.

The military camp in Nümmen near Solingen bustled with activity. Hans immediately ran off to report to his local commander while Helmut and I unloaded our bikes. Nobody seemed to pay attention as we wandered between tents and assorted buildings, tanks and trucks. More and more men surrounded the truck we'd arrived in, all of them keen to hear what was going on.

"Hans ought to hide," Helmut whispered. "When the Allies catch him, he'll go to prison or…"

"They'd shoot him for deserting."

"We better leave."

Helmut was right. We had no business of being here. I found Hans near the radio truck, where he was telling some of the other men what we'd seen.

"We're heading out," I said, suppressing the wish to hug him tight. "Take care of yourself."

Hans's eyes shone. "I'll come home as soon as I can."

As we hurried off, I noticed an open Kübelwagen near the gate. It stood alone and deserted, all men drawn to the radio news from the west. Dreamlike I stepped closer. The back seat held a dozen machine guns and Carbines, boxes and belts of ammunition. I grabbed a Carbine and handed it to Helmut, slung a machine gun over my shoulder, stuffed ammunition in my bag, all the while ignoring Helmut fervently shaking his head.

"You crazy," Helmut panted as we rode away.

Likely I was crazy. Any second one of the soldiers would call after us, demand us to stop. Guns would be drawn, we'd be arrested.

My legs peddled harder as my mind screamed to get off the road. We ducked into a path, crossed a field, then another. Forests and fields melded, though in my head I always knew what direction to take.

Four times we stopped to listen. But there were no shouts, no cars revving engines. Nothing but nighttime quiet with the occasional hoot of an owl or a rustle in the bushes.

At dawn we arrived in our neighborhood. Helmut took off down the road, the Carbine on his back. I tiptoed inside. Maybe Mother was still asleep.

No such luck.

She rushed toward me from the kitchen. "What happened?"

I froze. There was no hiding the gun. "Everything is fine," I managed.

"But you wanted to stay until Sunday and..." Mother's gaze fell on the weapon, still dangling from my shoulder.

"What have you done? Where's Hans?"

I shrugged. "Hans is fine...with his unit. We had to leave because the Allies were shooting at us, coming closer to the Rhine."

"Did you steal it from them?"

"It's from the Wehrmacht...in Nümmen."

Mother's eyes widened. "You must be out of your mind.

If they see you, the SS—"

"They didn't."

"Hide it, quick."

I wanted to argue, but at that moment the energy that had urged me to run from the allied attack and the reckless theft seeped from my body. I felt as drained as if I'd run for a week. I hurried to the hallway closet and hid the gun and ammunition belts between towels and sheets.

Helmut showed up in the afternoon and woke me from deep sleep. My earlier worries forgotten, while Mother read to my younger brother, I lifted the gun and followed Helmut outside. Luckily these days few people were on the road.

We took our bikes down the road into the woods.

After listening for movement or voices and hearing nothing, we began to fire our guns at the next best tree, a beautiful beech. The machine gun's recoil smacked painfully against my shoulder, the noise of the first shots deafening. Pop, pop, pop. And again. Pop, pop. The gun had a mind of its own, releasing salvo after salvo. My ears rang, yet I could not stop. The tree's bark tore apart as if it were made from paper.

The belt emptied. I tried another, while Helmut reloaded. We switched guns, continued shooting. Hollered and screamed.

Damn, that was fun. Stupid, but fun.

Until I remembered its purpose. The darn thing was meant for killing, not splintering tree trunks. What bravery.

As quickly as my elation had begun, as quickly it evaporated.

Helmut's enthusiasm seemed to disappear as well. "Can you imagine shooting on people?"

I didn't answer, all of a sudden worried, Hans may get

in trouble, if they found out his brother had stolen Wehrmacht guns.

"We better go home."

Wordlessly, I returned the gun to the closet, vowing not to try it again, unless it was a matter of life and death.

"I'm back," I announced, stepping into the kitchen, my eyes immediately searching for something to eat.

Mother was at the stove, stirring a white enamel pot, she used for soups. "Got a few onions and used those potatoes, you returned." She looked at me, a small smile on her face. "Maybe Hans will come to visit, now that he is stationed so close."

"If he gets leave—"

The doorbell rang. Not too many people visited these days, my immediate thought was that they'd come to arrest me.

Mother seemed to think something similar because she began to tremble. Only Siegfried, my younger brother, who was only eight and oblivious, ran to open the door.

Somehow, my legs refused to straighten. I remained seated at the table, trying to breathe normally. Impossible.

Voices rose in the entry. Mother spoke, then a man.

"Günter, you remember Helmut's uncle?" Mother motioned a man into the kitchen. He was tall and had the same curved nose as Helmut.

He studied me, his expression serious. "I'm here about the gun," he said without preamble. "Your mother told me, you are hiding it in the closet."

He half turned to Mother. "It's too dangerous, Frau Schmidt. The Wehrmacht or SS may see your son, or worse, the Allies make it here and consider your family enemies." He looked at me again. "Don't be a fool. I've got Helmut's Carbine, he told me about your shooting practice."

"Günter!" Mother cried. "How could you—"

"It's all right," Helmut's uncle said. "Nothing happened. But it's a dangerous game and won't end well. The SS executes people for smaller infractions."

He extended a hand. "Why don't you give it to me. I'll make it disappear, throw it into the Wupper River tonight."

I rose, slowly, half glad, half embarrassed and a bit angry about Helmut spilling our secret.

The gun had cooled and as I handed it over, I wondered if it had been used to kill anyone. The huge caliber would undoubtedly do severe damage. A shudder ran though me.

Helmut's uncle misunderstood and patted my shoulder. "It's all right, son, you are doing the right thing. Nothing good comes of this." Only now did I notice that he leaned on a cane. Helmut had mentioned something about a serious war injury. His uncle had spent months in a field hospital, had to learn to walk again.

"I'm sorry," I said quietly, unsure whether I meant Helmut's uncle, stealing, or losing the machine gun.

Only when he'd left did I breathe normally again. Had it only been yesterday that Helmut and I went to visit Hans.

As we sat to eat watery soup, my brother's image appeared in my vision. He could not go home and hide—like me. He was trapped in the military, trapped in that unrelenting war machine, that quashed people by the millions.

How much longer would the war continue? I looked at Mother and my little brother, the remnants of our family.

Would we ever be whole again?

Hans as a radioman

47 DAYS

The True Story of Two Teen Boys Defying Hitler's Reich

Solingen, Germany, March 5, 1945

I sat on my hands to keep them from freezing when our teacher, Herr Leimer, entered. After the citywide bombing last November when just about everything in Solingen had shut down, I'd finally managed to get back into a vocational school that accepted new students.

Leimer was old as dirt and had been pulled from retirement after all the real teachers had joined the war. It was March and our classroom, windows carefully plastered with assorted vinyl, cardboard and tarpaper, was as gloomy and cold as the frozen landscape outside.

Like my classmates, I wore a coat and a wool hat Mother had knitted from an old sweater. You could see puffs of breath rise from every desk. People coughed and sniffed, our noses red and dripping. Frustrated about the stiffness in my fingers, I had been opening and closing my fists because technical drawing was my favorite subject.

But instead of going to the board and suggesting a

quick-draw to warm up, Leimer repeatedly cleared his throat. His cheeks, rugged from age and too many cold nights—or as some rumored, too much drink—burned unusually red.

When the shuffling of chairs and bodies finally ceased, I forgot my icy hands. The old man looked as if he'd fall over any second. He even swayed a bit. Still, he didn't speak. Instead he looked at us with his watery blue eyes, holding everyone's gaze until the chair shuffling resumed and everyone began to whisper.

That's when Leimer raised his arms and the room turned as silent as a graveyard.

"Boys," he said. "I was asked to tell you…" Leimer's voice choked a little. "You've been summoned for another muster. Let me read what it says." He labored to unfold an official looking document, his hands bony and covered with bluish veins.

"Every man, born 1928 or 1929, must report for muster." He paused, his breath loud in the stillness. "If found fit for battle, your orders are as follows: Travel to *Marburg* by next Monday, March 12 and find the office of the Hitler youth." The paper sank. With it Leimer's voice. "That gives you a week. But first you have to report for muster to update your papers. Everything else will be explained there."

I scratched my jaw and took a look around the room. Had I heard right? I'd been mustered last fall and they told us then that we were deferred. Just a week ago Helmut and I had visited Hans, so we knew the Americans were only forty kilometers away…or less.

This couldn't be happening. Not now. I'd been sure the war would be over soon. Of course, nobody said it out loud, but at home people whispered of certain defeat. Last December when we'd met the horse soldier, he'd insisted the end was near.

A tremble went through me, starting at my toes and moving up and out through my limbs. I wanted to hurl my pencil at Leimer.

"How will we get to Marburg?" somebody asked.

"Where's Marburg? Are we all going?" Excited voices filled the room.

Leimer raised both arms. "Silence." The chatter subsided reluctantly. "There is no official transport to Marburg. It's maybe two hundred kilometers southeast. You must find the way yourself. Look for a truck or try catching a train. Most likely you'll have to walk."

"Why do we have to go now?" Paul Mans was still as small as last summer when the officer had slapped him around during muster. I was sure he dreaded another visit. So did I.

"The Führer needs everyone's help." Leimer hesitated as if he wanted to say more. But then he simply shook his head.

"What about uniforms?" somebody said.

"And weapons?" another boy yelled.

Leimer frowned. "I assume you'll receive everything when you get there. Class dismissed."

The room erupted in chatter, voices in various levels of development, deep baritones, mixed with scratchy adolescents. I watched Rolf Schlüter who always bragged and shoved people around. You were either in the Rolf Schlüter club or you weren't. I definitely wasn't.

Right now Rolf was surrounded by a throng of eager listeners. They all leaned in close while Rolf was explaining his strategy. "It's easy, you'll see. If we all do our part, we'll be there in no time."

Funny, I thought as I carefully placed the pencil stub in my pocket, Rolf is good at taking credit for other people's work.

Honestly, I couldn't believe how these boys could be excited. Had they not been around for the past five and a half years? Their chattering was getting on my nerves and all I wanted to do was leave—get away from them and their foolishness.

"What about you, Günter?" Rolf looked at me expectantly.

I swallowed a curse, forcing my expression into neutral. At least I hoped it looked that way. "I'll see if my friend, Helmut, is going. We'll head out together."

"Come on. Get your friend to join us. We're meeting in *Höhscheid* after the muster."

"Why there?" I asked, immediately regretting it. Now he'd think I was interested.

"Dieter says military convoys pass through all the time. We can catch a ride real easy."

How confident he sounded. "I'll try to make it, but I'm going to wait for Helmut," I said.

"What do you mean *try*?" Dieter asked. "You should be more enthusiastic. Didn't you hear the Führer *needs* us? This will be fun."

I attempted a smile though I wanted to shake my head. How could Dieter consider this war fun? Even a blind man could see that Germany was lost.

"Find your own way then," Rolf said. "But you'll look pretty stupid arriving days late while we catch ourselves some Russians." As if on cue, his friends laughed.

"My brother knows somebody in the *Partei*," one of Rolf's friends volunteered.

"My uncle is a major. He might know something," another boy chimed in.

How could these brothers and uncles be home when my father had been gone for years? Four years and ten months to be exact. And my brother, Hans, had left last fall. I didn't know much, but I knew that joining the war wasn't a smart idea. *You'd do what your father and Hans are doing. You'd be one of them.*

Standing back, I watched the group. Despite his strong words, Rolf looked small among his classmates. Several inches shorter than his friends, his voice didn't carry as if it were snuffed out by the bodies around him.

"I bet we'll arrive early," Rolf said. "Who is coming with me?" All hands in the group shot up. "Let's go and prepare. See you at muster." He stormed out, followed by his buddies.

I stayed behind along with Paul, who was slowly packing his bag. Herr Leimer still sat at his desk on the podium. He seemed to have aged overnight. I wanted to ask him what he was going to do now that the class had been dissolved, but then I remembered the muster. I couldn't be late, especially when it took forever to get there. The roads were still buried in rubble.

That afternoon I saw my classmates at the old elementary school where the military had set up another office. The other location had been destroyed during November's attacks. We all had to strip again and stand in line.

The commandeering officer looked grim as we stood shivering in the frigid air. This muster was even shorter than last time, the ancient doctor hardly looking at us. We all received marching orders to Marburg.

On my way home, I went to see Helmut. I knew immediately that he'd been to muster as well. His beaky nose looked even longer than usual and his cheeks were pale.

"I thought you might be stopping by," he said, leading the way to his room. He lived with his mother in a tiny white and black half-timber house in the old neighborhood of *Unnersberg* and had to lower his head in the doorframe.

"I'm not going. At least not immediately," I said as I plopped on Helmut's bed and told him about my lousy morning. "Remember the soldiers we saw in December? They said we should wait it out…that the war would be over soon. You heard the artillery fire of the Allies last week."

"I don't want to go either," said Helmut. "But we can't stay here. You know what they do if we get caught." His voice quivered as he sagged on a wooden chair by the window. He was usually pretty laid back, but this afternoon his forehead shone with sweat despite the chilly room.

"Of course, we can't stay, but we don't have to go to Marburg quickly. We could take it slow and wait. They said we should *try* to be there by Monday. How will they know who is going and how long it takes? I bet, they just estimate."

"You mean we hide?"

"For a while. See how things develop."

"What if someone checks our papers?" He got back up and began to pace around the room. "I'm not telling my mother. She'll go crazy with worry."

"She'll go crazy either way." I pushed away the thought of telling my own mother. "We could have *problems* and take much longer. Maybe I hurt myself. Or we get lost."

"You don't want to meet this Rolf?"

"No way."

Helmut grinned. "He sounds like an idiot."

"I'll see if we have a map. And food."

"Let's meet tonight around seven and be ready to go," Helmut said. "In case they're watching."

Sadly, it was true. One never knew who was trustworthy. With the deterioration of the country, hunger and desperation moved into homes and some figured a method to more rations was snitching for the SS or Gestapo.

I hurried home along the inky road, carefully picking my way. We hadn't had street lanterns in five and a half years, the city cloaked in darkness to hide from air attacks. Obviously, that strategy wasn't working because by now most German cities had been bombed.

With every step, the knot in my stomach expanded. I had to tell Mother. She'd already seen my father and brother leave for duty. Now it was my turn.

Determined to remain calm, I entered the kitchen and longingly looked at the scrubbed table. No pot sat on the stove. We barely ever had enough food to cook something warm these days.

I tossed my hat and gloves into the corner and called, "I'm home."

"You're late," Mother said, emerging from her bedroom with a patchwork-darned sock in one hand. She was a small woman, no more than five feet and I had the sudden impulse of hugging her to my chest. Of course, I did no such thing. I just stood there with my arms glued to my side. "I have cornbread and a bit of jam." She rummaged in the breadbox, the hollow sound echoing my stomach. "Better sit while you eat."

My belly growled as I slumped on the bench across from her. I was hungry, but then I was not. Had she heard? I searched Mother's face for clues, but she showed the usual strained face from years of holding together her fears.

I forced air through my throat. "I've been drafted." How weird that sounded.

The darned sock dropped on the table. "What do you mean?"

"We got mustered a second time and I'm ordered to report to Marburg."

"What? Today?"

I nodded, hoping my voice remained strong. "I'm supposed to go to Marburg on my own. My entire class does. Helmut, too. I've got a week." I swallowed the last of the bread. The crumbs stuck in my throat and I gulped down a glass of water. I got up, keeping my lips pressed tight. That's how Hans had acted when he left.

"But you're barely sixteen." Mother's eyes were dark with tears, her small hands holding on the edge of the table. "Do they want to kill us all? You have to be careful, Günter. Promise me."

I nodded, resisting the urge to climb onto her lap and bury my head.

"*Mutter*, listen." I sat back down and took her fingers in mine. "I...we've decided we won't go straight there. We'll take a really long time. We'll go slowly, walk around in circles. You know what they said...the war should be over pretty soon."

"But we don't know when." Mother squeezed my fingers. "You *must* be vigilant. The SS...they'll shoot you on the spot if they even suspect—"

"Don't worry, we'll make it," I said, wishing my voice sounded more convincing—to her, and to myself. I straightened abruptly and headed to my room. Time to pack.

"Will you see Father and Hans?" My little brother, Siegfried, hovered in the doorframe. He was only eight and seemed tiny to me, a latecomer surprise to our family.

I hurried over and kneeled in front of him. "There are lots of men out there, but I'll definitely look for them." How could I explain to my eight-year old brother that I had no intention of following my father and brother? *Traitor*. They were out there fighting a war that was long lost and what was I going to do?

Siegfried leaned his cheek against my shoulder. "Will

you write?"

I squinted my eyes shut to keep them from leaking and patted his back as an answer.

DAY ONE

It was dark when I snuck out of the house. Mother was tearful but quiet, clutching Siegfried to her chest. I swallowed repeatedly, the knot in my throat the size of a soccer ball. All the words I'd wanted to say didn't come. All I could think of were my burning eyes and my damp palms until I thought I'd choke. Had father and Hans felt the same when they'd marched off? I abruptly turned and closed the door.

It was an unusually cold night for early March, the ground frozen solid. Helmut waited at the corner, his breath steaming in the air. A half-moon colored the sky in burned orange and purple. Scattered clouds threw shadows across our path.

We walked silently, each carrying a small sack with a set of extra clothes, a blanket, some bread and a few potatoes. It was hard to comprehend we'd not go home tonight or any night soon.

I hadn't found a map, so we headed south into the woods. Somehow, we'd have to find road signs and watch the sun for direction. Leaves rustled underfoot and a frigid wind blew. We'd hiked the *Wupper River* hills a thousand times, the landscape as familiar as my backyard. I'd never realized how much I'd loved it here. How I'd taken things for granted.

"You all right?" I said to distract myself.

"Sure."

"You don't sound *sure*."

Helmut didn't answer.

"Why aren't you talking?" I couldn't keep the anger from my voice.

"What about?"

"Idiot."

Suddenly, Helmut stopped and hurled his pack to the ground. "Who are you calling an idiot? Have you thought what happens if they catch us? Everyone is heading to Marburg. What will they do if we don't show up?"

"We just have to hide. If anyone asks, we say we got lost."

"What if we're wrong? How do you know the war will be over soon? I mean it's been going on for five and half years. What if it continues and they'll find out we…" Helmut lowered his voice. "We'll get executed."

"Shut up. The way you're going, we'll be dead in ten minutes." I wanted to smack Helmut in the nose. "I don't know what's going to happen, but I know that I don't want to go. People are dying everywhere. Everyone…" I swallowed to push away the thought of my brother and father, "is getting killed. This is stupid."

"I say we go close to Marburg. And then wait."

"Wait for what?" I scratched my forehead. "For the SS or the Russians to find us? Sit in the bushes and watch the action?"

Helmut remained silent.

"We should stay in the area and go where there're fewer people. We can always head to Marburg later."

Helmut didn't answer, but he picked up his bag and began to walk.

The trees grew denser and darker as pines and cedars mixed with oaks and beeches. We found shelter in an old hunting stand about six kilometers from home. The small box, built on twenty-foot poles overlooked a field, was one of thousands sprinkling the landscape. Not daring to make a fire, we huddled in the corner, the wind claiming free reign through the open window.

I couldn't sleep, nor could I feel my toes. It was early morning, the hour before dawn when thoughts of hopelessness and doubt whisper. Dew soaked my hair and blanket. I tried pulling my coat across my knees, but it was too short. I'd grown again over the winter.

Above me, branches moved like giant fingers. Something rustled on the ground below, the sounds magnified by the darkness. The knitted gloves Mother had given me allowed too much airflow, so I stuck my hands between my legs. I longed for my bed, the familiar sounds of home, and my mother. I dozed, but sleep refused to come.

Helmut had a point. What if we were wrong and the war continued much longer? Never mind the handful of soldiers we'd met who whispered of certain defeat. Who knew what was true? All we heard came through the radio, the barrage of announcements, the constant flyers. Not that I listened anymore—at least not on purpose.

What if we were stopped by a patrol? Or we ran into Russians or Americans? We had no weapons and no training. Not even enough to eat to last a couple of days.

I shivered.

At dawn, it began to drizzle. I looked over the fields, trying to decide on a direction. Two deer grazed below, beautiful and out of reach. Helmut was leaning back, his mouth relaxed in sleep, his wool cap covering one eye.

I punched my friend in the arm. "We better go."

"Let me sleep," Helmut mumbled, turning in search of a more comfortable position. Unable to find it, he opened his eyes. "*Scheiße*, I'm freezing."

"Get your lazy butt moving then." I was in a rotten mood. Helmut was capable of sleeping anywhere, day or night, while my own mind refused to shut off.

Heads low, we trudged into the countryside. The land rolled in soft hills and wide valleys, sprinkled with forests and open spaces, and dotted with an occasional farm or village. The wetness softened our steps but crept beneath our clothes. We walked carefully, avoiding streets and houses, jumping off the road as soon as we heard a sound.

Sometimes, we found a barn filled with straw or hay and crept inside after dark. It was easier to find or steal a bit from a farm. While most farmers had to deliver their harvest to the cause, they always seemed to have reserves. After all, it was easier to grow and hide food when you had land and outbuildings.

DAY SEVEN

Hard to believe we'd slogged around for a week. Helmut and I had been friends since elementary school, but I was growing tired of his company. I knew he felt the same by the way he squinted at me. We hardly spoke and when we did, we mumbled some words, each encased in his own misery.

"I wonder when we can go home," Helmut said as we walked along a narrow trail. Ferns sprouted, their rolled stalks unfolding through last year's layer of leaves. The forest felt empty, void of anything edible except for the animals we couldn't catch. A ray of sun appeared, adding sharp colors but no warmth to the afternoon. What did I expect? It was only the middle of March.

I'd had the same thought, but kept my mouth shut. By hiding and avoiding others, we had cut ourselves off from any news. We ran around blind while somewhere south, the Americans were creeping closer. In the east, the Russian Army was moving toward Berlin.

What if *Solingen* had been bombed again? What if something had happened to our families?

Last November the Brits had flown a weekend attack,

leveling the city. Downtown had burned for a week and when we'd gone to take a look a few weeks later, white sheets fluttered where bodies needed pickup. Along the sidewalks the dead had been stacked like cordwood, the stench of decomposing bodies a toxic cloud taking our breath.

Ever since I'd avoided thinking about the carnage, but now that we were away, I found not knowing was torture. I pulled off my cap and scratched my head. Everything itched.

"Let's rehearse again and make sure we say the same thing." I couldn't help myself thinking about being caught. It was as if a thundercloud followed me ready to strike.

"We're going to Marburg?" Helmut volunteered.

"Maybe we should say we got turned around. Lost our way in the woods."

"We better say I turned my ankle. Who's going to believe we're lost for a week?"

"All right. Fine." I couldn't keep the irritation from my voice.

"If we'd followed *my* idea, we wouldn't have to constantly think of different excuses. We'd just wait in the wings."

I bit my lip. Maybe Helmut was right. But the thought of going south and getting near the very people who would execute us if they knew made me shudder. "Let's wait a little longer."

Helmut sighed, a deep rumbling sound. "You think the others arrived?"

"They might already be shooting people." I imagined Rolf with a rifle, his face covered with mud, taking aim at an invisible enemy. I thought of Paul Mans, the small boy who always seemed afraid even in class. Doubt crept up in me, and I abruptly left the trail.

"Where are you going?" Helmut yelled after me.

I shrugged and scratched my neck where the wool coat had left a circle of raw skin. I had to distract myself. My armpits reeked and my crotch itched. We'd soon pick up lice or some other vermin if we didn't wash. But that wasn't what bugged me. The aimless wandering was driving me crazy. Helmut's frown was driving me crazy. Worst of all were my own indecision and doubts.

With a sigh, I thought of my bathtub. Even if I had to haul water and warm it on the stove, it had been pure luxury compared to living in the woods.

"You want to wash?" Helmut's expression was incredulous as if I'd suggested flying to Africa. Helmut dipped a forefinger into the water. "Liquid ice."

I ignored him and stared at the stream that gurgled across moss-covered rocks. This early in the year, the water was knee-deep. Light reflected off its surface in brilliant colors. Ordinarily, I loved all bodies of water, had built plenty of dams in the creek in front of our house. But I'd only gone swimming when it was hot. I pulled off my coat and sweater, unbuttoned shirt and pants, shed shoes and socks, toes curling against the cold dampness of a long winter.

The air pierced my skin. Goose bumps spread. Helmut didn't move.

"Are you going to watch or what?"

"Fine." With a sigh Helmut tossed down his bag and tore off his jacket.

I turned my back and waded into the stream, splashing myself. "Damn, it's freezing." My feet were numb, making it impossible to keep my balance. I slipped and took a dive.

My ears filled with ice, my lungs bucked. Now I understood what 'mind-numbing' cold' meant. Even after two winters with no coal, I'd never frozen like this. I frantically pulled my legs beneath and straightened with a splash.

Helmut was down to his underwear, his lips blue. "We don't have any towels," he stuttered. His collarbones stood out, his ribs lined in perfect order below like the keys of a piano. Why had I never noticed? Before the war we used to go swimming to the public pool. A lifetime ago.

So, why go on? Why not lie down right here, right now? Or better yet, march to the next Hitler Youth office to turn ourselves in. I couldn't answer that question. All I knew was that I'd continue as long as I could walk. I had to believe a new life waited somewhere beyond the horizon. What was another day or week after five and a half years?

"I can't wait to take a real bath again," I said as I rubbed myself down with my shirt, pulling the spare underpants from my bag. A thousand needles pricked my feet and legs and, had it not been for the hollowness in my middle, I'd felt refreshed.

"Let's go," I said as soon as Helmut was dressed.

My urge to move was greater than my need to rest.

DAY TEN

Ten days had passed and we were getting into a routine. Every time we reached a road, we watched and listened for several minutes before crossing, only to disappear into the next thicket. With the forest virtually void of food, farms and fields were the only place to score: a handful of potatoes or rutabagas, sorrel and half-rotten apples, a few soggy grains. Not daring to make a fire, we chewed our few finds raw.

We hiked cross-country until we came upon a small, well-kept farm far back from the road. I scanned the grounds for signs of political expression, a swastika or the German flag.

There were none. The house stood quietly. Not even a rooster crowed.

"Let's ask for food," Helmut said.

"You think it's safe?" I scanned the windows of the farmhouse, imagining eyes behind the curtains. The home had red brick walls and clay shingles. The modest barn next to it showed two low-rising stalls. Nobody was in sight.

We rehearsed quickly... on the way to Marburg, got lost, needing supplies to get there.

I knew Helmut was afraid by the way his upper lip trembled. Just in the last two days I'd noticed my own legs turn shaky. It was like walking on half-cooked spaghetti. My stomach hurt most of the time, and I had trouble sleeping even though the nights had been warmer.

"You want to ask?" I whispered.

"Maybe we should wait till dark and look for something to steal."

"We need to eat," I hissed. Anger reared inside me like a vicious animal, another side effect of starvation. Yet, I didn't move either.

"We better find out how many people live here," Helmut said, settling himself against a tree stump.

Out of nowhere a dog the size of a German shepherd raced straight at us, black fur bristling. It growled and showed impressive white fangs.

"*Guter Hund*," I whispered, feeling my leg muscles tighten, wondering if we could afford to turn our backs without being eaten for lunch.

The dog drew closer, paws silent on the packed dirt, its snarl vicious. As I began to tremble, Helmut cried, "Move slowly and climb the tree."

An old man materialized in the entrance of the farmhouse and pointed a rifle at us. "What do you want?"

"I wonder if you could..." Helmut said.

"Spit it out, boy. I don't have all day."

"We're hungry...and unarmed," I offered. That was technically untrue, because I never went anywhere without my pocketknife. My knees remained frozen in place.

"Up to no good, are you?" The man waved the rifle and took a step closer.

"We just wanted to ask for something to eat," Helmut said. "We better go."

"Not so fast. Come out of that bush and show

yourselves." Had the farmer's voice softened or was I hallucinating?

"Hungry, eh?" he said as we slowly approached.

I kept one eye on the dog, which had stopped growling, the other on the barrel of the gun. I felt Helmut next to me and considered giving him a sign. But whether to run or advance was anybody's guess.

"Come here, Rudi." The dog trotted to the old man, tail wagging.

"I can see you haven't eaten in a while." The old man's gaze came to rest on our mud-covered boots. "A shame what this country is coming to." He shook his head and walked inside. I hesitated and looked at Helmut.

"What are you waiting for? Come in," the farmer said. "Take off your shoes."

The kitchen looked worn like the man's knobby hands, but the oak table was polished clean. The man set his rifle in the corner by the sink. "Let's see what we have," he mumbled as we halted halfway into the room. "Sit, boy."

Was the old fellow talking to his dog or us?

The man rustled around his cupboards. "Sit down, boys." He nodded at the table.

We sank on chairs across from each other, my throat dry and my stomach knotting with hunger and worry.

In front of us paradise unfolded: dark rye bread, butter, cheese, homemade jam and dried sausage. It was impossible to tear my eyes away. Helmut gulped saliva.

"So, who are you?" The farmer's eyes, sunken within the folds of lose skin, were hard to read.

We're in hiding, I wanted to say. We're running away from the war.

I sighed with relief, hearing Helmut say, "I'm Helmut. This is my friend, Günter. We're on our way to Marburg to enlist."

The farmer studied our faces. "How old are you?"

"Sixteen," we both said at the same time.

The kitchen turned silent. Somewhere in the corner, wood settled in a stove. I was trying to breathe shallowly. My hands shook under the table. All I could think of was the food in front of me, and our lie hovering like an evil ghost in the kitchen.

Strawberries, my brain announced as a whiff of jam slammed into my nostrils.

"...better be careful?" The old man's eyes were on me.

"What?" I said.

The old man shook his head as he sagged on a bench next to us. "I said you boys are much too young to fight. You must be careful."

I nodded slowly, watching the old man's expression. Things sat between us. Unspoken things, yet I was no longer afraid.

I reached for a slice of bread and forgot our misery.

The man watched in silence as we stuffed ourselves. At last I leaned back with a sigh. We'd said little, the old farmer's face relaxed, his eyes twinkling beneath the shadows of humungous gray brows.

"You can sleep in the barn if you want. Just stay out of sight during the day."

I nodded, pulling my gaze away from the bread. My stomach bulged and yet I wanted to eat more.

"I'll give you breakfast and something for the road tomorrow." The old farmer nodded and straightened with a grunt. "Promise me to be careful."

I attempted a smile and shook my head. The man sounded like Mother. Better not think about home. Not now, not any time soon.

But when we sank into the hay, which smelled fresh and felt warm to the touch, and the wind's whispers lulled me away, my thoughts wandered to my parents and Hans, and how they were all scattered. I longed to be with them.

In the beginning, I'd counted the number of days: 192 days since my father left, 166 days since Hans had been drafted, 97 days since I'd last eaten a decent meal. Now, where my father was concerned, I counted in years.

Most of the time I didn't count at all.

DAY THIRTEEN

We stayed two nights, helping the old man with cleanup, stacking wood and straw. On the thirteenth day, with bread and cheese in our bags, we were headed south again on one of the main roads when I heard the rumbling of engines.

Jumping over the embankment filled with a foot of brackish water, we slid into the dense brush. I peered through the leaves as the ground began to vibrate and the noise grew to a roar.

A German military convoy crawled toward us at a snail's pace. Cars, horses, wagons, trucks and people clogged the road. The men looked grim, their uniforms filthy. They shuffled along on foot. The luckier ones were riding high on top of flatbeds. Many were injured.

I couldn't help but scan the men's faces inside the medical trucks. I saw their dulled eyes and bloody stumps. How still they lay. Some moaned. I felt relief when no one looked familiar. Maybe my father was long dead, lying frozen and forgotten in some mass grave.

"You think we should show ourselves?" Helmut said into my ear.

I shook my head as I stared longingly at the provisions trucks and wondered if these soldiers knew about Marburg. All it took was one zealous officer and we'd be turned in.

DAY FIFTEEN

"I want to go home," Helmut said two days later as we
hiked yet another forest path. "We're starving, and my
shoes are falling apart."

"What if someone sees us?" I said, trying to ignore my
own eagerness for a warm bed.

"We'll be careful."

"Just for a day, then?"

Helmut nodded, a grim smile on his face.

It took us two more days to reach our neighborhood.
Everything seemed to be the same and I breathed a sigh of
relief to see my house standing solid in the dark. I snuck
through the basement door and tiptoed my way upstairs.
Muffled voices drifted into the hall. I had to be absolutely
sure nobody saw me. I tried the entrance door. It was
locked.

"Who's there?" Siegfried asked from the other side.

"I'm back," I whispered. The door flew open. I slipped
inside just as Mother ran from the kitchen.

"Günter!"

With a sigh I relaxed into her warmth.

"What're you doing here?" she said. "It's not over, is

it?"

"No, *Mutter*. But we overheard some soldiers—the Americans are already in *Siegen.* The Army is retreating everywhere."

Mother shook her head. "You can't stay. If someone sees you..."

"I know." I'd never wanted anything more. "Have you heard..." From father and Hans I'd intended to say, but my voice didn't obey.

"Nothing, no letter." Mother avoided my eyes and hurried to the breadbox. "I'll fix you something to eat."

Like I'd done at the old man's farm, I closed my eyes as I ate the cornbread. Mother seemed thinner than two weeks ago and I wondered if I was eating her ration. Still chewing I walked to my room. My bed looked warm and inviting. I wanted to curl up and sleep forever.

Mother followed. "You better stay in the basement. I heard the SS just shot several people for picking up leaflets."

"What did the flyer say?" I asked, wandering back into the kitchen.

"That we should surrender when the Americans come." Mother sagged on the bench. "Hitler wants to kill us all first. Promise me to be careful. I'll get you an extra blanket."

When no footsteps or voices could be heard above, I quietly opened the entrance door and snuck downstairs. I was hungry again, but that couldn't be helped. I locked myself into the coal cellar and spread out on an old mattress we kept down here for bomb alarms.

I awoke from the rapping on the door.

"Better get up," Mother whispered. I unlocked and snuck upstairs. After the warmth of my bed, the kitchen felt like an icebox. "We're short on wood," Mother said as if she'd heard my thoughts.

It would've been easy for me to scrounge firewood, but I couldn't risk it. The SS often appeared out of nowhere, and many people had disappeared after being turned in by spying or opportunistic neighbors like the man who'd stolen our horse last December. With a sigh, I pulled on my coat and sat down to a piece of cornbread and peppermint tea. I left the next evening at dusk, picking up Helmut on the way.

The beginnings of spring tinged bushes and trees with fresh green. We kept hiking, some paths familiar, but it was hard to tell anymore. Entire forests were disappearing, either bombed and burned or cut down for firewood.

DAY TWENTY

I could never get used to the cold. No matter how fast we walked or how we wrapped ourselves in coat, hat and gloves, the wintry air crept into my bones. First, it sat on top, just a whiff as if somebody breathes on your wet skin. You shiver a bit, but get distracted and forget.

But the cold doesn't stop there. It is sneaky and mean as it knocks past the skin and climbs inside you. There it spreads with thousand tentacles until your insides freeze and your muscles stiffen and ache. Shivering is no longer an option, it's a must. You have no choice. That's when you get scared to fall asleep and die of hypothermia. When you jump up and windmill your arms to pump the slush in your blood.

Whenever I got this cold, I thought of home. I couldn't help myself. Mother's soups came to mind, the red-hot stovetop in the midst of winter, fed by the comfortable heat from the seasoned roof trusses we scavenged from bombsites. I'd thought it had been hard after the bombing, the 'Angriff' last November when Solingen burned down. I'd been angry about the additional work fixing the roof and our windows, having no running water or electricity.

Now I knew that even the little we'd retained, had been comfort. Mother and Siegfried had been there. I'd slept in a bed and sat at a table.

Out here in the hilly land I'd always loved and considered familiar, I was at a loss, a drifter at the whim of a madman.

Another thing I noticed was the quality of time. In misery, time has a tendency to slow down. Every minute stretches, an hour feels like four and a day lengthens into a week. Your thoughts turn in circles, cloud your perception.

On day twenty we found a frozen bird, some kind of pigeon with grayish white feathers and clouded eyes.

"You think it's still good?" Helmut poked the rigid body with a stick.

I bent low to sniff. Nothing but earthiness hit my nose. The bird's body was intact. "Let's try a fire and see."

We were on a hillside overlooking a patch of evergreens so we headed into the woods to better hide the fire.

The bird was hard as an ice cube, so we laid it on a rock beside the flames. Luckily, there was little smoke because the evergreen trees had produced plenty of twigs, many even dry.

"Wonder what it tastes like," I mumbled as I turned the bird yet again. Its neck was soft now and lay at an angle.

"I'm going to gut it," Helmut said. "Used to help Father clean rabbits," he continued, his voice dreamy.

I watched as he positioned the bird on its back and slit it open from neck to belly. Innards burst from the cut. I swallowed and made myself busy feeding the fire.

"I think it's all right," Helmut said, rubbing his hands with pine needles. He'd cut off head and feet too.

Relieved, I quickly carved a stick to a point and skewered the bird, trying to ignore the thought of worms and maggots slithering inside.

"Wonder what it died from," Helmut said as we took turns holding the bird above the fire. The air reeked with the stench of burning and melting feathers.

"Old age?"

Helmut stared at me and then ever so slowly his expression grew into a smile. A giggle rose from my throat, so strange and yet, so good. Helmut followed and soon we were laughing so hard, my ribs ached and Helmut sputtered for breath.

The aroma of roasting meat made us stop. Our gazes turned to the pigeon as if we were hypnotized. I couldn't look away, my mouth flooded with saliva. I wanted to rip the thing off its skewer and sink my teeth in and it took all my self-control to remain sitting on the wooden stump.

"Come on, get done already." As usual, Helmut echoed my feelings.

Oh, hunger, you nasty brother. Always present, always nagging. Didn't we have enough worries already? Yet, Russians and Americans, the SS and assorted fanatics paled when it came to an empty stomach. In a way, hunger was a mightier enemy than people. Like the cold, it was sneaky and quiet. Always present, always on your mind. Causing pain in places you didn't know you had. Hunger shoved aside logical thoughts, our prudence we so desperately needed. It would almost cost us our lives.

Helmut carefully cut the bird in two pieces and we feasted.

DAY TWENTY-THREE

The light was fading and we still hadn't found a suitable place to sleep. Usually, we scoped out an area during daylight, so we knew what to expect. But our vigilance was waning. I often daydreamed to escape the gnawing fury in my middle. At least it wasn't raining and the forest floor, soft with fir needles, buffered our steps. The pleasant sharp smell of sap lay in the air and I took deep breaths.

"Damn, I don't even see a hunting blind," Helmut said over his shoulder. He was a couple of steps ahead, his voice deeper than I remembered, though he was as skinny as ever.

"Or a barn."

"Let's hurry then—"

"Can't see more than five feet with this stupid undergrowth." Indeed, this part of the woods hadn't been cleared or picked clean and brush and blackberry bushes tore at our clothes. The terrain was leading downhill into a narrow valley. Somewhere ahead water gurgled.

Likely that meant no people. It meant safety, but it also meant nothing to eat.

We were climbing across a pile of mushy tree trunks

when I heard a rumbling. "Wruff, wruff."

In the waning light it was hard to tell where the sound had come from.

Helmut froze and turned to look at me. I shook my head. Puffs of white breath rose between us. My mind sped up. Was there a road ahead...snipers...the SS? I felt the blood rush through my neck. My hands were clammy, damp, neither hot nor cold. Looking at my friend kept me from running, kept the panic in my bones contained.

Above us fir boughs whispered, but the forest held its breath—the silence absolute.

"What *was* that?" Helmut whispered.

I shrugged. "Let's hurry before it gets totally dark."

We jumped off the log pile when all hell broke loose. High-pitched squeals mixed with deep grunts as a wild sow broke from between two trees not six feet away. In the twilight she was almost invisible, her gray coat shaggy, her small eyes on us.

"Run," Helmut cried, the panic in his voice almost as frightening as the angry sow.

Where to, I wanted to say, but it was too late. The sow rushed me with such power that I smashed to the ground. Wet leaves hit my face, followed by searing pain. My calf screamed and a moan filled my ears. I don't know if that's what scared the sow away or if Helmut's crazy shouts from the top of the log pile stopped her. He'd climbed back up and stood there like an apparition, waving a huge tree limb.

I wanted to laugh because he looked so funny but that's when the pain crawled up my thigh into my hip and down to my toes. *The sow bit me*...bit clear through my pants and socks. It hurt worse than when I tore my shin in the barbwire a few years ago.

Helmut's face appeared above me. He was pale, the fuzz above his lip damp.

"She's gone," he panted. "She had young. We scared her." I followed his gaze to my leg where a dark stain spread along my calf.

"Damn," I cried.

I sat up with effort and I leaned forward. I didn't want to look, but my eyes were drawn to the darkening spot. Helmut gingerly lifted the seam of my pants. Even that slight movement sent me through the roof. Air rushed from my throat in a gasp.

Helmut kneeled closer. "Hold still," he said. I couldn't see the wound very well because the bite was on the right backside of my calf and it was growing seriously dark now. "We've got to get you to a doctor," he said quietly. I heard the concern in his voice. In a way it worried me more than his usual loud complaints. "You might need a shot of something...maybe stitches."

I grunted in response because the throbbing was growing stronger—even overpowering my hunger. A gurgle rose from my throat, sort of a mix between laughter and a sob.

"I guess I've got an excuse now," I said.

"What?" Helmut sounded exasperated.

"I mean, if they ask us why we didn't go to Marburg."

Helmut mumbled something and held out a hand. "Come on, I'll help you."

When I straightened, the pain expanded again. It was a live thing with a pulse like its own heart. Putting weight on the leg made the pain grow further. I thought of the soldier with the missing arm who we'd helped cut wood. Losing a limb had to be infinitely harder.

We stumbled forward, each step a challenge. It was getting even harder to see and my leg had a mind of its own. In front of us the gurgling grew louder.

The creek was tiny, no more than three feet. Ordinarily,

I would've jumped across, but now I stepped smack in the middle, soaking my right shoe. Freezing cold joined the thumping in my leg.

When I stumbled, I felt Helmut's arm on my side. By the time we reached the top of the hill, it was dark. Ahead lay a narrow road, reflecting a bit of moonlight. We began walking. *Let them catch us*, I thought. *At least I'd be able to lie down.*

I didn't know how much time had passed, but at some point we saw lights ahead. Those were joined by other lights. Nothing bright like a city, more like a village.

Helmut helped me lean against the entry door of a modest home before he deftly stepped to the entrance. In the overhead light, the door shone bright green. I took it as a good sign.

I didn't hear much of the talk, my focus on the pain that was taking over my body.

A shadow appeared next to me, then another and I felt myself lifted.

"Let's put him in the spare room," a woman's voice said. "I'll go and get the doctor."

I didn't know if a minute or an hour passed, but at some point an older man bent over my leg. He asked for more light and a pillow before rolling me on my side and propping up my leg.

I wanted to scream then, felt my forehead grow damp, then wet. The wall in front of me was white with little specks of gray like the footprint of tiny feet, so I focused on that.

"I've got to wash it clean," the man said.

"Here, bite on that," the same woman said. A washcloth appeared in front of my face and I took it between my teeth.

The next moment I wished for my leg to disappear. A burning sensation drilled into me, expanded until it knocked on my bones. I wanted to kick...kick away the pain, the scraping soreness. But somebody was holding me still. I couldn't see anymore because my eyes were filled with tears that slipped past my nose into the pillow.

Oh, how I had wished to sleep in a bed. Just not this bed. Not this way.

"Should be good now," the same voice said. "I'll sow it up."

Tugging and a slight squeaky sound traveled to my ears. My mind was all foggy, but I heard that sound as loud as the live band we used to listen to in town.

I must have drifted off because when I awoke grayish light trickled into the window. With a pang I remembered last night, the scary sound, the sow's attack.

My leg throbbed dully, but not nearly as bad. I was covered with a feather comforter though the room was very frigid, my face cold.

I carefully touched my leg. It was bare—they'd taken off my pants—except for a bandage around the calf. I wiggled my big toe. Not too bad. But when I tried to move my ankle, the pain woke with it.

I lay back with a groan.

"You awake?" Helmut's sleepy voice drifted up from the floor. Seconds later he was by my side, hair standing on end. "Doctor says it'll be an ugly scar, but you'll be all right."

Despite the pain I smiled.

DAY TWENTY-SEVEN

We stayed two days with the kind woman before taking off again. She'd repaired my pants and shared her meager supplies, but we were worried about her neighbors. The doctor who turned out to be a retired veterinarian had visited twice to sniff the wound and change the bandage. I was supposed to remove the five stitches in six days.

Anymore, I was losing track. The first three weeks I'd counted every day, but the monotony of our journey was softening my brain.

"It's been four weeks," Helmut said as if he'd heard me. Like some old married couple, he often said what I was thinking and vice versa. We were hiding inside an abandoned barn, its walls nearly collapsed around us. "What do you think Rolf is doing right now?"

"Wonder." I inspected my fingernails. They reminded me of the chimneysweeper who was always covered in soot and came by the house twice a year to remove coal dust. It had been in another century.

"I think we made a mistake," Helmut said, avoiding my eyes. "I mean, not going down there."

"Don't know." I imagined my classmates exploding with shouts and applause as Rolf Schlüter, his chest full of medals, marched into class. "I hate not getting any news," I managed.

"What if the war continues another year?"

I grimaced and jumped to my feet, the sudden move making me wince. "I don't know." I was so tired. Tired of Helmut voicing the same questions and doubts I had myself and couldn't answer. Tired of being hungry and most of all, tired of being afraid. "Why don't you send a letter to Hitler and ask him what he plans?" I sneered. The anger was choking me like the insides of the bunker.

"I just mean I can't go on like this. My legs ache all the time." Helmut's voice had turned to a quiver.

"We'll have to." I punched the rough wood of the barn with my fist, welcoming the immediate pain. "How many times can you be lost? It's too late to show up in Marburg, even with the new scar."

"It's all your fault," Helmut said heatedly. He began to pace back and forth in the empty barn, his cheeks smoldering. "We should've gone down there. I shouldn't have listened to you." He threw up his arms and abruptly stopped in front of me. "You said the war would be over soon. But it's not. What if Hitler wins?"

"He won't."

"How do you know?"

"You heard what the soldiers said. You *saw* them—all torn up…retreating."

"Men say lots of things. People tried to kill him over and over. He always survived. Maybe he *is* invincible."

"He's like any other man, except insane."

"Why don't you admit that you were wrong?"

I shrugged. Maybe I was, but judging by Helmut's fury and balled fists, I wasn't about to admit it.

"Should have and would have," I scoffed instead.

Helmut sagged onto a pile of moldy straw. "You might as well have pulled the trigger. It's only a matter of time before the SS finds us. Or the Gestapo or one of their spies—"

"Shut up! Just shut up," I yelled. "I'm tired of your complaining. Why don't you go back and turn yourself in?"

I didn't want to admit that I felt just the same. My own legs were killing me, the sow's bite a dull throb. My stomach cramped most of the time and I felt surrounded by permanent darkness.

Helmut didn't leave, but after that we no longer talked. We took cues from each other, stopped to pee or take a break. I found myself listening to his breathing and his sighs, the way he cleared his throat. I wanted to say something, but the invisible wall between us held like reinforced concrete. We never looked at each other and we never spoke.

And with every day we got more exhausted until our gait resembled that of old men shuffling and dragging across the woods. We rested more, but the cold weather wasn't finished and we soon had to move again. A few times we risked a fire, the damp wood smoldering and giving off little heat. I worried about the smoke being seen.

More and more convoys clogged the roads. Plain soldiers snaked along in unending streams. I wasn't as afraid of them now because I knew they had little to do with the SS and Gestapo.

"Go home, boys," they whispered when we watched from the side of the street. "We have no ammunition left. The Americans are close."

How close, I wanted to shout. *How much longer?* All I did was nod, afraid to get into a discussion about our wanderings, afraid of looking at Helmut's face. We saw women pushing wheelbarrows with bedding, coffee grinders, pots and assorted suitcases, worn grandfathers with packs and children...small ones with thumbs in their mouths, some school age like my brother Siegfried.

Everyone looked hungry and frightened.

DAY THIRTY-FIVE

At last, we got brave enough to hitch a ride on one of the military trucks of a German convoy. Well, that is, I moved out into the line, hoping that Helmut would follow.

"Hop on up, boys," said one of the soldiers walking past. He smiled grimly through the muck on his face, his uniform jacket splattered with dried dirt.

So we scrambled onto one of the trucks, feet dangling over the edge.

"Did you see the truck behind us?" I shouted over the engine noise, somehow emboldened by our ride.

"No, why?" Helmut yelled back, his attention on one of the soldiers plopping down by the side of the road. The man's boots were torn and he was in the process of taking one off. The sock underneath was dotted with holes.

"They're loaded with food, you know, military bread."

"*Kommissbrot?*"

"We should ask for some." Without waiting for an answer, I jumped off the platform, immediately regretting it as a dull ache shot up my right calf. After passing two vehicles, I noticed a soldier marching alongside with his hands on a rifle. That had to be it. Sure enough, the provisions truck was stacked to its tarped ceiling with dark square loaves like shoe cartons.

"You think you could spare some bread?" I asked, thinking that it felt good to hear Helmut's voice.

The soldier, not much older than I, shot me an appraising look. "Two loaves. We aren't going to slow down for you."

I glanced at the tall truck and the broad tires ready to squash me. I'd wait. "No problem, thanks." Then I yelled over at Helmut, "We can get some, but I'll have to wait to climb up till they stop or slow down enough."

He made a face and kept silent. Stubborn idiot.

When the road turned steep, the caravan decelerated to a crawl. The guard winked as I took hold of the back ramp and pulled myself up. I carefully selected two loaves and stuffed them in my shirt, making sure not to upset the load. Though the *Kommissbrot* was dry and hard, the whole rye, wheat and molasses would fill our stomachs like a real meal. I wondered if the rumors were true that they contained sawdust.

A shout made me look up. Like in a movie, the soldiers a few hundred yards back were jumping into ditches and running for the trees.

That's when I grew aware of a buzzing sound, growing rapidly louder as if someone had unleashed a giant nest of hornets. Gray specks appeared in the sky. They grew larger quickly—a squadron of low-flying enemy planes. Before I had time to act, machine gun fire exploded and the back of the convoy dissolved into a cloud of dust.

Terror crept up my legs. The shooting sensation of adrenalin hit my gut like a fist. I was in the open, ten feet above the road, a perfect target. There was no time to climb down and find Helmut on the other truck.

I jumped…flew…

Rat-a-tat-tat-tat…The ground rushed up to me. I rolled into the ditch as the sky darkened above me. Bullets shredded the bread truck, pierced tarps and metal with ease. I covered my head and lay still. My right calf throbbed—the noise was deafening. All I could do was lie there and wait and hope that none of the bullets or shrapnel found me.

When the blasts subsided, I sat up, noticing with relief that I was unhurt. Many others hadn't been so lucky. The sounds of human suffering drilled into my brain—men moaning and crying. My first impulse was to run. Run as far as my legs would carry me.

That's when I remembered Helmut, and cold panic seized me. What if Helmut had been shot? Unable to control my shaking hands, I scanned the road. Soldiers lay strewn between broken-down trucks like throwaway dolls. Most lay still.

I recognized the friendly guard from the bread truck a few feet away. He was on his back, eyes wide open, staring into the sky. His helmet had flown off, and the top of his skull was gone, reddish gray oozing onto the pavement.

Another man lay on his side near the ditch crying softly, "Help me." The front of his army coat had blown to shreds, his intestines visible. I tried to look away, but the man stared straight at me. Since I was still in the ditch we were at eye level.

The man had blond hair, shaven around the ears, his eyebrows brownish caterpillars that didn't match the reddish tinge of stubble on his chin. Blood gurgled from his mouth, and he sputtered as if he were under water. At last, he stopped moving, his gaze frozen.

I climbed out of the ditch. I had to find Helmut. In my confusion, I couldn't remember where I'd left him. My heart raced worse than when I'd run sprints in school. I hurried along the road, turned this way and that. I recognized the truck we'd been on, now broken down, shot to pieces. The wooden bed had splintered, its tires flat. Helmut wasn't there.

"Helmut?" I cried, voice high in my throat.

Men were running and shouting orders, checking for wounded and dead. I dashed around the broken-down truck. I checked the ditch. No Helmut.

With every step I grew more convinced that Helmut was dead and that I was alone, an island among the frantic activity around me. Until I couldn't walk any farther. I stood amidst the chaos, my mind blank, my body paralyzed.

"Günter?" Helmut's voice drifted through the fog. "Over here."

I turned on my heels, watching uncomprehendingly as Helmut rushed up to me. Mud stuck to his right cheek and temple, but he looked whole.

"I went to look for you," Helmut panted, his eyes huge in his face.

I searched for my voice. "I couldn't find you," I croaked. "I thought you were…"

Helmut patted me on the back, a grim smile on his lips. It was the first I'd seen since the pigeon roast. "I'm all right."

I grinned back, then glanced at the sky. "Let's go. They may return."

We melted into the woods, the bread securely tucked in our jackets. During the night, I dreamed about the man with the reddish stubble. In my dream, the soldier sat up, pulling feet of intestines out of his belly. He laughed crazily as he kept piling them on the ground.

I awoke, my face sweaty and cold. I looked to my side where Helmut slept under a blanket. Only a few strands of sandy hair were visible. For a moment I felt intensely thankful that my friend was safe. I wanted to reach over and touch his shoulder, tell him that no matter what we'd stick together. It was the only thing that mattered, the only thing Hitler would not take away.

I sat up and broke off a piece of bread. It tasted metallic, as if it were tainted with blood.

DAY FORTY

Nearly six weeks into our journey and after finding nothing but rotten potatoes in a deserted field, we reached a small village about sixty kilometers from home. A pub was the only official building. No matter how small a village, every place had at least one tavern.

Having no industry and being tucked into the hills, it seemed the war had passed this town by, at least as far as we could see. Houses and sheds were intact. Even the church steeple with its bronze bell, white stucco walls and a modest stained-glass window was unharmed. Several military trucks and jeeps parked a couple of hundred yards down the narrow street.

"You think they'll give us something to eat?" Helmut asked, sounding doubtful as we stared at the whitewashed walls of the *Gasthof Zum Löwen*. Lights shone from the inside, coloring the windows in a warm glow. The delicious aroma of roasted meat drifted across.

I tasted bile, and my insides churned. We hadn't eaten since yesterday, a handful of shriveled onions from last year. Risking a fire, we'd thrown our find into the wood coals and gulped them down half raw.

"Wait here, I'll go."

I stepped into the street. Nobody was around, though I suspected the trucks were well protected. Trying to keep up my resolve, I slipped into the pub.

With the low ceiling and darkly paneled walls, it felt as suffocating as a bunker. Thick smoke hung in the air. After the brightness of the evening sun, I squinted in the gloom.

A fat man in a black shirt and stained blue apron stood behind the counter, wiping up beer spills. The smell of something sour mixed with stale alcohol filled the air. I wondered how the man could serve food and liquor while nobody else had anything left.

Afraid to lose my confidence, I deftly stepped to the counter. Too late did I notice the military jackets.

I would've recognized the emblems anywhere: a jagged double S clearly visible on collars, armbands and hats: SS officers.

Three men occupied stools to the side of the bar, smoking and talking loudly, a selection of empty glasses in front of them. I silently swore as I glanced back at the entrance, my hunger forgotten.

To my horror, the room fell silent.

"What can I get you?" the barman said, his deep-set eyes black raisins within folds of doughy skin.

I licked my lips, scolding myself for being sloppy. Why hadn't I peeked through the windows first? Now it was too late. I stood smack into the middle of a nightmare.

If I screwed up now, we'd be done for. I *had* to appear confident.

"My friend and I are looking for a small meal," I said, forcing air through my lungs. "We don't have money, but we can work."

"Another beggar." The barkeeper addressed the

officers with a mock grin.

Ignoring the men in the corner, I shook my head. "We'll work for what we get."

"Let's hear him out," one of the officers said.

"What can you do?" The barkeeper asked with a detached voice.

"Chores," I stammered, "like dishes, cut wood, or we can repair stuff. I'm good at fixing things." I looked around the room in search of an obvious item in need of maintenance. The silence grew. I could feel the officers' eyes burning into me.

One of the men leaned forward. "What about fixing our country?"

The officer next to him chuckled. "It'll take more than hammer and nails."

I noticed that the third man hadn't joined the laughter. He looked irritated, his eyes gleaming as coldly as distant stars. Unsure what to do and afraid they'd ask more questions, I stumbled on, "We can work first and you can give us food afterward, as payment."

Why didn't I just shut up and leave? The SS and their obvious arrogance meant nothing but trouble or worse. As I stood rooted to the middle of the pub room, the officers began to whisper.

"Oh, come on, barkeep. Give the boy a break." One of the officers came over.

I did a double take. The guy looked like an older Birdsnest, the boy who'd tormented me in the Hitler Youth a thousand years ago. He had the same blond hair, shaved along the sides, leaving a tuft of curls on top. I couldn't be sure. Five years had passed, but for a moment I worried if Birdsnest would recognize me.

"Here, I'll pay for his dinner." The man tossed down twenty *Reichsmark*, something I hadn't seen in a while. The bartender mumbled but took the money. "Better get your comrade, then. Looks like you have a new friend."

"I'll be right back." Now was my chance to disappear. Fast. I turned on my heels and sprinted off, colliding with Helmut outside the front door. Trying to control my panic, I frantically blinked at Helmut, furious with myself for neglecting to set up a distress signal.

"How did it go?" Helmut asked innocently. "I am soooo hungry, I could eat a house."

"I don't—"

"Hello there," someone said behind me.

I flinched. *Breathe.* Luckily, I had my back turned. Helmut's eyes widened as the blond SS-man in the immaculate uniform, the high black boots waxed to a perfect shine, stepped into the street.

"What're you waiting for? Your food is ready."

I managed a nod, my throat too tight to speak. *Run away now*, my gut urged. *Run and you'll be shot*, my mind argued. We had to play along. Either way we were dead.

The barkeep appeared as soon as we sat down in one of the booths by the window, his huge stomach hidden behind a white porcelain bowl and plates. "Enjoy."

I swallowed and reached for the ladle. The dark venison stew smelled heavenly. I wanted nothing more than to eat, yet my belly churned with fear. Helmut looked almost green. We had to talk normally or raise suspicion. I managed a weak nod and filled my plate.

To my relief the barman reappeared, shielding us from the SS men. "Bread and beer, courtesy of your new friends."

I eyed the glass before nodding in the general direction of the counter. I wanted to be drunk and forget everything. But alcohol made you careless.

"May I have some water, please?" I asked, my voice foreign in my ears.

I knew the officers were watching us, so I grabbed the fork and slowly began to chew. The rich sauce exploded in my mouth, my taste buds doing overtime. The bread was warm and the crust thick and fragrant. I forgot the men and our situation, my stomach demanding to be heard.

Amazing how you could still eat when your head was already in a noose.

I watched Helmut who was chewing hard, his eyes glazed. We kept eating until the last of the stew had disappeared and the breadbasket was empty. I leaned back and belched. My stomach roiled with a mix of cold fear and too much food. Why hadn't I thought of an excuse to leave? I was just thinking of what to say to Helmut when Birdsnest materialized at the table.

"*Obersturmführer* Kummel, may I sit?"

It *was* Birdsnest. I cleared my throat, hoping that my voice didn't wobble. "Nice to meet you."

"Thanks for dinner," Helmut offered, his gaze hanging on the officer a moment too long. Helmut had made the same connection.

"Where are you boys headed?" Birdsnest asked. I stared at Helmut, trying to decide what to say. Helmut's cheeks were as pale as the tablecloth.

I've got to say something. "We're going to Marburg. Trying to get there on foot."

"Show me your orders!" Birdsnest held out his hand. I scrambled to find my papers. What if the officer asked where we were from? How could we be north of where we'd started when Marburg was quite a bit south?

Instead of studying our papers, Birdsnest jumped up. "Did you hear that?" he asked, addressing the officers at the bar. "These two are going to Marburg."

"You don't say." Another officer approached our table. "Didn't they give the order to Marburg weeks ago?" He scratched his head.

I froze. This time it wouldn't be pushups—this time we'd be lined up outside and shot. To my surprise, I still breathed, my clammy palms under the table, my feet cold, toes rubbing against the leather. Why didn't I just fall over and lose consciousness? Get it over with?

"...is your lucky day," the officer was just saying.

"What?" I croaked, coming out of a daze.

Birdsnest jumped in eagerly, "We're heading to Frankfurt. You can hop in the back of our truck and," Birdsnest paused, "Harald, you don't suppose we can take a little side trip to drop off these fine young soldiers?" The third officer, who scrutinized us without speaking, stood up.

"I'm sure."

Birdsnest, now with a proud note said, "You see, you'll get to fight very soon. We need every man."

I choked and hurried to cough. Looking up from my plate, Harald's arctic eyes met mine. Forcing my mouth into a smile, I glanced at Helmut whose upper lip trembled.

"Harald, isn't that great?" Birdsnest chuckled. But Harald didn't speak—he kept staring at me.

"That's wonderful," I blurted. "When are you going? We're pretty tired. We walked all day."

The second officer nodded toward the ceiling. "We sleep upstairs. Meet us here at 05:30."

Birdsnest stood up, snapped his right arm into the air, "*Heil Hitler!*" The other officers followed suit and we raised our arms.

"A little more enthusiasm, perhaps?" Harald wandered over, his voice high, almost girlish.

"Ah, leave them alone." Birdsnest slapped his comrade on the back. "They'll learn soon enough. A few weeks of training and they'll be ready to take on the Russians."

Harald nodded but kept staring as if he wanted to

decide whether to shoot or cut us into pieces.

I straightened, thankful my legs were holding up. "We better rest so we'll be ready for the trip."

"You can sleep over there." The barkeeper pointed to a side room with tables and benches. "It's hard but I guess you're used to that."

"We'd be happy to sleep in your shed," I suggested. "We don't want to take up any space." I hoped we might escape if we were outside the building. Especially since it was getting dark.

"No need boys." The bartender smiled. "I'll make room for the young soldiers of our fatherland."

"Thanks," I managed. I had to buy time. We couldn't run out. That would surely raise suspicion. This fellow Harald looked as if he'd enjoy shooting us on the spot.

"We better find the outhouse. Do you have water outside?"

The barkeep pointed to the back door. "Through there, take a right. The outhouse is straight back. There's a faucet next to the house."

"Come on, Helmut." I headed to the backdoor, hoping to look enthusiastic. To my horror, the barman followed and ambled past us.

"Right over there is the latrine. And here's the water."

Without another word, I entered the outhouse. Sweat dripped underneath my shirt. *Breathe.* The stench was overpowering. I needed time to think, but there was no quiet spot. It'd be suspicious if we stayed out too long. My head was numb. The more I tried to concentrate, the more panicky I felt.

I stepped outside, slamming the door shut. Helmut was leaning against the house, his eyes wide with panic.

"Now what?" he whispered, his voice shaking with anger. "Why did I listen to you? They'll find out as soon as we get to Marburg. Maybe even earlier…"

I just shook my head, my eyes imploring Helmut to be quiet. Somewhere above us a window opened. Our worst nightmare was coming true.

We'd be taken to Marburg and then we'd be executed. I thought of Mother, imagined her pacing the silent apartment, stopping in front of the empty beds. I opened the faucet to cool my burning face. The water was freezing but I didn't feel it. My gamble had failed. Tomorrow we'd die.

To my relief the officers had gone upstairs when we reentered the pub.

"I'll bolt the doors." The barkeep didn't wait for an answer and the room grew dark. We were locked in.

Heat and cold took turns on my skin. My throat tightened, the feeling of an invisible hand choking the air out of me. I was back in the bunker…in…out…in…out.

"Listen," I whispered, concentrating on every breath, "we have to disappear before morning. If they take us down there, it's over."

Helmut leaned closer. "If they catch us fleeing, we'll be dead, too."

"We'll leave between two and three. That should give us enough time to safely disappear."

"But the doors are locked. How will we get out."

"Through the windows."

"But where are we going? What if they follow us? Or somebody is outside watching? They probably have guards." Helmut's whispers grew louder. "It's all your fault."

"Shhh!" I hissed. "We'll go south." I was mad at Helmut for talking and saying the things I'd been thinking. Most of all I was mad at myself for letting my guard down, for allowing my hunger to lead us into danger.

"They won't expect that," I said. "We'll keep away from

the roads. One of us has to stay awake. We'll take turns. There's a clock in the main bar. You take the first watch. Wake me in two hours. It's nine now. Do *not* fall asleep."

Despite my sluggish mind and the unaccustomed beer I'd been too weak to refuse, I had trouble relaxing. I worried about Helmut falling asleep or worse, telling the officers. What if he turned me in to save his own neck? Impossible. We'd been friends as long as I remembered. The bench creaked under Helmut's weight. I nodded off.

I dreamed my father walked into the bar. He was smiling and ordering rounds of beer for the SS men. A hole gaped where his stomach had been. He was laughing as he tipped his drink, beer pouring from his middle. I screamed and awoke.

The first thing I noticed was that I was freezing and the second that I couldn't see Helmut in the darkness.

"What time is it?" I whispered.

Nothing. *What if he's gone to tell the officers*, the voice in my head commented.

"Helmut?" Relief spread as I detected even breathing nearby. Remembering the clock, I carefully tiptoed into the main bar.

With one hand outstretched I felt my way to the counter. The clock was somewhere on the wall. I walked along the bar, running my hands across the top where I'd seen matches yesterday. Even in the dark I could tell that my hands shook. My fingers caught on the matchbox and the phosphor exploded into flame.

Raising the light toward the clock, I blinked. It was four-fifteen. We'd slept more than seven hours.

Panic gripped me. Fingertips burning I dropped the match. It turned dark as my mind began to race. Any minute the men would be up. I hurried back, shoving Helmut in the shoulder.

"Wake up."

Helmut yawned. "I fell asleep."

I wanted to strangle him. "It's really late."

Helmut grumbled. "What time is it?"

"Hurry," I whispered, "from now on not a word. We'll head straight through the backyard."

"Fine," said Helmut, making the bench creak all over again.

Groping in the dark, I found the window latch and pushed. I'd thought about our escape route last night. With the doors locked, windows were our only chance.

The window didn't budge.

What if the frames had been nailed shut? I hadn't thought of that. We'd be locked in.

Again, I lifted the handle. Something screeched, wood scraping against wood. I pushed harder.

The window reluctantly gave and I held my breath to listen. Any sound would travel. What if the SS had men stationed around the inn? Surely there were guards somewhere close. My breath rattled in the silence. The air outside was windless and absolutely still while my heart pounded in my head so loud that I was sure they heard me upstairs.

I lifted one leg across the sill. Carefully shifting my weight, my foot hit the ground outside. Something crunched and I froze. Ever so slowly I added more pressure. Something beneath my foot broke like a firecracker. New panic rose in my throat. *Run.* I pulled the other leg out quickly and threw myself into the darkness, hoping to land on something soft. Watery grass blades hit my face.

"Wait." I scrambled to my knees and rummaged across the ground. I couldn't see Helmut, but heard his movement in the window. Something jagged cut my hand, a piece of glass or shard, some forgotten flowerpot. I managed to pull away my fingers just as Helmut's foot hit the ground. Again I listened.

All I heard was Helmut's labored breath and my own heart pounding in my neck.

I looked up where I knew the second floor windows to be. It was impossible to tell if any stood open. If someone upstairs couldn't sleep and stood by the window, he would certainly hear us. That grim officer, Harald, was creepy, kind of sinister. I had no doubt Harald would execute us.

I shivered.

The air smelled damp and thick with wetness. It clung to my skin, penetrated my coat, and turned my fingers stiff. Not daring to speak, I stretched one arm to the side, touching Helmut's shoulder. The other hand reached straight ahead. I tried recalling the landscape behind the garden, vaguely remembering trees and bushes. Why hadn't I paid better attention?

A dog barked in the distance, a detached sound, ghostly, impossible to tell how far away. I heard Helmut suck in air, his fear palpable in the darkness. *You've got to be strong.* I carried on, one step...another. It was impossible to tell where we were going. If we wandered off course, we might run straight into a guard or one of the military trucks. I willed my ears, all my senses to lead us.

There was no room for error. Not now. I couldn't let it happen. My thighs wanted to cramp, weak and shaky at the same time. Still, I placed my feet carefully, moved in painful slowness.

A terrible stink reached my nose as my fingers touched something rough. The outhouse. We'd only made it a few yards.

A door slammed behind us and my knees gave. I dragged Helmut with me. A light danced toward us. Somebody shuffled across the lawn. Any second we'd be seen.

We crept around the outhouse away from the light. A loud yawn reverberated, a door squeaked, followed by the unmistaken sound of things dropping below. I tried holding my breath to avoid smelling the stench. I wondered if it was the barkeep.

The dewy grass poked my skin like icy fingers and I began to shiver. The barkeep would find us gone and tell the SS men. Why hadn't we closed the window to make it less obvious? I was too stupid.

I hardly noticed when the door slammed and the man moved away. He noisily scratched his body as his shadow dissolved into blackness.

Helmut punched my shoulder. "Let's go."

We straightened and wordlessly, one shaky arm outstretched, stumbled forward. It was like walking into a void, a black hole with nothing to guide us, every step a new risk. Brush slapped my face and I closed my eyes. It was just as well. Every minute seemed like an hour, every step a mile. My knees were soft with dread.

Without warning, my hand struck something firm—bark. We went around, stumbling across roots and stones. Another tree rose up. And another. What if we were going in circles?

"Can we rest for a minute?" Helmut whispered.

"Only a minute." I fell to the ground, not caring about the spongy wetness.

"How long do you think since we left?"

"We haven't gone far enough." I envisioned the nasty officer barking orders, saw dogs sniffing, teeth bared and then—

"I wish it were light," Helmut said. "I hope we're heading in the right direction."

"We better go."

After a few feet we ran into another tree. Limbs rustled above, a whisper—it had to be a forest.

Another dog barked. It seemed farther away. We kept walking, last night's dinner a faint memory.

Helmut abruptly stopped and cried, "Ouch, my hand," just as I felt something sharp digging into my waist.

"Barbed wire." I cursed the darkness, blindly feeling for more wires. There were three, the lowest a foot above ground.

"Where do you think this is going?" Helmut asked. "Maybe we should walk around."

"Better go straight," I said, imagining a mad bull charging us on the other side. Cows were a thing of the past. If there were any, the farmers hid them well. "I want to go as far as possible from the inn."

"Wonder how far we've come," Helmut said again.

He always says the things I'm thinking. We've been together too long. But then I remembered the bombers and how I'd thought I'd lost Helmut. And I knew then that I'd rather stick with Helmut until I couldn't walk another step than to spend one hour alone. "Slide across the ground. I'll hold up the wire," I said aloud.

Helmut dropped to his knees and scooted low. "Now you."

The grass was an icy bath as the wire scraped across my back. The trees had ended which felt like walking in space. We had no reference, no direction. Only the ground sloped lower.

"Let's wait here until dawn," I finally said.

The grass was short with tough blades, the ground squishy and I soon began to shiver. Faintly in the distance we heard sounds.

"You think they're looking for us?" Helmut asked.

"Don't know. You'd think they have better things to do

than chase a couple of boys."

"Hope so."

When dawn broke, we found ourselves on a former pasture. Behind us, the land rose toward the trees. Ahead, it fell into a long valley, a patch of woods to our left.

"Let's hide in the forest," I said. Continuing toward the trees, I fought the urge of looking over my shoulder.

We collapsed in the gloom of a pine stand. Needles covered the ground, and the air was filled with the sharp aroma of pine tar. How I longed for a fire. We were drenched with a mixture of sweat and dew, the skin on our hands hard and dry, fingers bony, knuckles scraped bloody.

I wanted to be home, take a hot bath and go to bed with a warm comforter and clean sheets. I thought of the other beds, my father's and my brother's which had been empty much longer.

Lately, I'd been having a hard time remembering my father's face. Everything was turning blurry, even the memories of how life had been before the war. I thought of Mother standing in the kitchen, looking at Siegfried, the last child, the last person at home and I longed for her embrace, her smile or even her scolding look when I'd forgotten to do a chore.

DAY FORTY-SEVEN

Helmut sat up from his makeshift bed underneath a hazelnut bush. It was too early to carry fruit, but the fresh green was thick. "I want to visit home. I could really use a bed for a day or two."

I jumped up. "That's the best idea you've had all day."

Seven weeks had passed since we'd left for the woods. It seemed a lifetime ago. Now that I thought about it, I couldn't stand living this way another second—even if it meant being home for a few hours.

We hiked cross-country until I recognized the hills of the *Wupper* valley.

"Did you see that?" Helmut pointed at a couple of houses in the tiny village of *Wupperhof*. "They have white sheets hanging out the window. You think somebody died?"

"Maybe." I thought of the city bombing last November when white sheets had signaled dead bodies ready for pickup.

Pushing the thought of swirling flies and decomposition from my mind, I concentrated on the happy face Mother would have when she saw me. I couldn't wait to see her.

"I don't know how much longer I can do this," Helmut sighed.

"It should be over soon. Remember what the soldiers said." How often had I repeated these words? Rolf Schlüter returned to my memory, showing off his medals in class, sneering and pointing his pistol at me. *Deserter*, he said. *Arrest him.*

I walked faster. Anything was better than to think about the consequences of my actions. I was blind to the fact that spring had finally arrived. Though the leaves from last winter rustled underfoot, the trees were bright green, bathing us in shadows.

"There's another sheet," Helmut said, panting and holding his sides. "Do you think they have some kind of disease? The house isn't bombed."

"I can't imagine what it would be."

"What about typhus—you get it from bad water."

"Maybe they poisoned the wells or the reservoir." I kept walking. "If the Americans and Russians are close..."

"What're we going to drink?"

"We'll have to get water from a stream and boil it." What if Mother had gotten sick and died? I hadn't been home in weeks. Lots of things could happen, sometimes within an hour or a split second. I quickened my pace.

"Slow down!" Helmut massaged his ribs, panting. "I'm tired."

But I couldn't stop, even if my legs burned and my throat had turned to sandpaper. I had to get home. Now. Never mind it was daytime. That we were in plain sight.

By the time we arrived in the neighborhood, my lungs ached, and I was wheezing.

"Let's meet again tomorrow night. I'll pick you up after dark." I didn't wait for Helmut's answer and sprinted up the street. On *Weinsbergtalstraße* I slowed down—then sighed.

The apartment houses still stood.

But the street seemed strangely deserted, and I noticed more white sheets. There was my house. Finally. I scanned the windows of my family's apartment. Nothing. But wait. There was a sheet on the side. I hadn't noticed it at first, but something white hung on the side of the building, my parents' bedroom.

Mother had died.

Dread crept up my spine like icy fingers, urging me to sprint the last bit. The apartment door was locked and I retrieved the spare key from under the mat, something Mother and I had agreed upon when I left.

"*Mutter?*"

Nothing. As my eyes adjusted to the gloom I ran, checking every room—the apartment was empty. They'd taken Mother away. Siegfried was probably dead, too.

I sat down heavily, a deep sob building in my chest. Pain spread through me like acid and burned a hole where my heart had been. I'd wait here till the SS picked me up or a bomb fell on me. I glanced around the clean and orderly room, my father's favorite leather chair. It'd been empty for five years. Now I was truly alone.

Tears streamed unchecked. Time stood still.

Images of my family danced in my head: eating a meal, Mother baking a pie, my father repairing an outlet, Siegfried galloping around the house, pretending to be a horse, Hans lying on his bed reading a book. They kept circling, drawing me in, a swirl spinning faster and faster, pulling me down and away. The air turned black and thick as molasses—too hard to breathe.

Would my lungs simply stop? After my experience in the bunker when I had experienced claustrophobia for the first time, I'd often thought about choking to death. It made you want to jump out of your body for fear of drowning.

"Günter?" Mother plunked down her water buckets and rushed to my side.

I looked up, taking in Mother's slight figure, the patched coat and the scarf wrapped around her head. Was I dreaming? Only one way to find out. I jumped up and threw myself into Mother's arms.

"Am I glad to see you," I choked.

"Are you all right?" Mother held me tightly. "What happened?"

"I thought you… the sheets in the window."

"Oh, you thought…" Mother shook her head. "This time it's not a sign of dead people. You didn't hear?"

I stared. What was she talking about?

"It's over. The Americans are in town. Solingen has surrendered. That's why we have the sheets out." Mother touched my cheek.

"The war is over."

I watched Mother disappear into the kitchen, yet all I could see was Helmut's dirt-smeared face, the way he'd looked after the bombers almost got us on the road.

It's over. Over.

No more hiding. No more running through the woods, afraid of meeting the wrong men. After six years, Hitler's foul veil had been lifted. Never again would I need to hide in the basement or sneak out after dark. Helmut and I could walk the street without that creepy feeling somebody was watching.

"Better come and eat." Mother's voice drifted into my consciousness. "Afterwards, I could use some help with firewood."

As I got up to join my family, a chuckle burst from my throat.

I was finally free.

Of course, that moment didn't last. Happiness is but a fleeting emotion. Like a blast of hot air in a cold room, it tends to vanish. As postwar Germany began, it ushered in new pressing questions. How would we survive in the rubble when there was no food, no work and no money? But most of all, what had happened to Father and Hans?

Günter as a young teen   Günter after the war

A LIGHTNESS IN MY SOUL

Introduction
In the fall of 2019, my friend Marion called me, her voice equally excited and urgent. She had been in a repair shop in Herten, Germany, where she lives. For Germans this ritual comes twice a year when we change our set of tires for winter and then again around Easter for summer.

Of course, that wasn't the exciting part. While waiting on a less than comfortable plastic chair, a fluorescent light overhead throwing shadows on the gray linoleum, piles of dog-eared magazines about cars and sports resting on a side table, she had noticed an old man sitting quietly. He wore a flat gray cap and, though it wasn't exactly cold yet, a checkered wool scarf curled twice around his neck.

Except for a curt nod, he hadn't spoken. Only when my friend mentioned the constant need for tire changes, had he focused his watery blue eyes on her.

She didn't recall how they got to the subject of war. But at some point, in that barren waiting area, he told her he'd been in the *Kinderlandverschickung* or KLV for short, a program instituted by the Third Reich, sending German children and youth to safe areas in the east or south and out of reach of allied bombs. Marion mentioned her mother who'd also participated and not enjoyed it one bit.

The old man seemed glad that my friend was familiar with the program. He commented that it was sad the world tended to immediately suppress and forget such terrible history. He'd hesitated and then continued, that he'd always done the same. After a moment of silence, he'd turned his attention to my friend and asked, "You have a moment?" The old man's wrinkles deepened and his eyes began to glisten with tears. "Let me tell you a story," he'd said, "one I haven't told anyone my entire life."

Fixing his gaze on my friend, he began, "I was fifteen, when the war ended..."

He made a strange face, one so full of pain and upset that my friend felt compelled to ask, "Wasn't that a good thing...I mean that it was over?"

Shaking his head, he continued, Marion listened, and soon they both cried.

My friend didn't tell me all the details—which of course, I would've loved knowing—just the framework of the man's ordeal. And though she later tried to find him again, she was unable to.

So, I took it upon myself to recount the old man's tale with as much historical and detailed information I could find. I do not know his real name—I named him Arthur—but I know that the world ought to hear his story.

GERMANY, JUNE 1943

When I first heard the word camp, I envisioned a place of great pleasure, relaxation and good food—in short, a sort of extended vacation. That's what we were told when our class set off to spend a few months away from home.

But that word—camp—is versatile in ways I'd never imagined. It is a loaded word, so harmless sounding, so innocent.

Nothing could be farther from the truth.

The children's evacuation program, KLV, had grown since Hitler called it into existence in 1940. By June 1943, many cities were carpet-bombed by the Allies. The formerly voluntary program became a required one because our school was ordered to send its classes into the KLV.

That's why our class traveled to Bavaria to get—the way our teacher, Herr Wagner, put it—away from the bombs.

I'd resolutely ignored Mother's sighs when she rifled through our stash of ration coupons or studied the daily obituaries of fallen soldiers in the paper. Though she was rather upset to see me leave—my father was fighting somewhere in France and after I left, she was alone—I was looking forward to spending time away.

A former orphanage, repurposed as a boarding school for boys, squatted tall and square as an oversized shoebox at the outskirts of a small village. On clear days, the Alps loomed so close one could watch the wind hurl snow drifts into the clear blue sky. The place was basic: large dorm rooms for ten or twelve boys, except for the leaders, who each had their own space. Our washrooms were old with squeaky plumbing and moldy patches on the walls. Once a week, we bathed in a tin tub with hardly enough water to get wet, a far cry from the Saturday baths I'd taken at home. The squabbles, the noise and the lack of privacy were grinding.

The Hitler Youth ran the camp, and even Herr Wagner had to follow their orders. He was pretty strict, a tall, skinny guy with a stern mouth, his hair short and stubbly with graying temples. He'd look at you with those deep-set eyes and you'd shut up. But the camp leader, a fellow named Steinmann, outdid him by far. He didn't even have to look to get his point across. When he showed up we all hushed, including our teacher.

How he did it, I don't know. He wasn't even particularly tall; in fact, most of us towered over him. But that didn't seem to stop him from doling out punishment when he saw fit. And that was daily. His favorite was marching and standing at salute for hours at a time.

Half of Steinmann's face was burned, leaving a pockmarked, scarred landscape that was rumored to be a war wound he'd suffered in one of the early battles in Poland. It made his face lopsided, having obliterated his right brow altogether. They say our eyes are windows into the soul, and that was the first time I believed it: Steinmann's eyes were a metallic gray, cold and distant, and a little bit dead.

Steinmann kept a tight rein on the camp, the first hour spent cleaning shoes and rooms, folding and refolding our laundry, flag hoisting and eating an increasingly meager breakfast. After lessons that lasted until noon, we trained for war, an unending succession of running, pushups, person-to-person combat, wrestling and of course, marching.

We used sticks and tackled each other, laughed when Otto Mainzel stumbled and face planted. Otto wasn't exactly fat, rather large-boned with a face full of freckles that continued over his chest and back in uneven patches, made worse by the coarse carrot hair that refused to be tamed. Otto was the least sporty of all of us, which was evident even when he walked, a sort of stiff-kneed saunter. For the most part, we despised him. Those who didn't outwardly demean him, ignored him.

Among us, there was much talk about heroes and our future roles defending the fatherland.

"When I catch myself an American, I'll show him the meaning of brave," Udo Bauer exclaimed after a particularly heated exercise with sticks. He was taller and fitter than most, almost six feet, and his skin glowed pink beneath the shorn hair above his ears. Most of us wore our hair in such a way—Steinmann made sure the village barber visited monthly—but Udo also parted his, which was blond and straight, on the right like the Führer. I'd long given up trying, because my curly hair had other ideas.

"We'll arrest them or better yet, shoot them," Hans Heiden sneered. He was Udo's best friend or dare I say *only* friend, and always copied Udo's moves.

We were sitting around, cooling off on a green patch behind our home that doubled as parade ground, soccer field and meeting place.

In the beginning, I thought we'd be home before Christmas. After all, wasn't the war going well? The Führer said so, and the newspapers were full of victory reports.

But in early December Wagner told us that it was too dangerous to return home. The Ruhr river region, where we'd grown up, was not only one of the most densely populated in Europe, it was famous for its productivity. Mining and steel fabrication, chemical industries, but particularly the production of tanks and artillery made our area a preferred target for the British Royal Air Force.

I was no longer excited to be away and missed my mother terribly. Every letter she sent, I carried around with me for days. The few times she mailed me packages— usually with homemade cookies, a pair of hand-knitted wool socks and last winter, a scarf—I'd extended eating those cookies for weeks, just to preserve the joy of receiving a piece of home. For the last several months, mail and packages had all but ceased.

Of course, that wasn't something we mentioned to each other, each of us wary and determined to appear strong and brave. Only in the dark of night, lying awake on lumpy mattresses, did we allow ourselves to weep. I knew I wasn't the only one, but by morning I was careful to extinguish any signs of fragility.

SUMMER 1944

By the summer of 1944 we were demanding openly to go home. Every time Wagner shook his head, his lips pinched, his gaze far away, as if he wanted to avoid looking us in the eyes.

"It's been a year, why can't we go?" I asked, feeling fed up after another bad night. My best friend, Emil, had a cough and a couple of boys cried out in their dreams.

"It isn't safe, Arthur." The muscles on Wagner's neck tightened as he stared off into the distance, yet his gaze seemed to go inward as if he wanted to hide.

"That's what you said last Christmas."

Usually, Wagner would've snapped back something, but today he remained strangely calm. "Believe me," he said, his focus returning to us, "I'd like to go home as well, but we must wait."

"If we're winning the war, why isn't it safe?" asked Emil, who had a sharp mouth on him when he wanted to. Two years ago he'd moved into the neighborhood with his grandmother and joined my high school class. You know how you meet somebody and instantly like him? You don't know why, just that you're comfortable and somehow connected. That's how it was when Emil showed up. Even if he was crazy superstitious and constantly made predictions, which luckily for the most part didn't come true.

Wagner seemed to search for the right words. "We've got to be patient."

"I wish we could fight them," Udo announced. "Why are we doing all this training, if we never use it?"

I wasn't so sure I wanted to have anything to do with fighting battles. It was one thing to play fight with sticks, another to face American or Russian tanks.

"You may get your wish," said our teacher. Once again his gaze wandered off, once again I had the impression he wanted to say more, but kept his thoughts to himself.

Two days later he was gone.

SPRING 1945

The spring of 1945 arrived with colorful patches of dandelions and forget-me-nots. The air was thick with the scent of mowed grass, which took me straight back to my home and the countless times Father had made me help in the garden. Homesickness hit me in the gut as I thought of the way our lives used to be—five long years ago—before Father had left for the war. The feeling was so strong, I wanted to curl into a ball and hide beneath the bedcovers as I half-listened to the squabbles of my classmates.

"I'm surprised they haven't drafted us," proclaimed Udo, the only one standing. It was getting harder and harder to exercise when we didn't have decent dinners afterwards, so the rest of us sat or lay on our backs in the grass. Udo's cheeks burned dark as blackberry juice and his hair stuck to his forehead, but he seemed determined to appear invincible.

"Maybe we lost, and they forgot to tell us," Emil said. Just yesterday, he'd seen two gray field mice which according to him were a sign of doom.

Quick as an angry hornet, Udo marched over to us and

punched his own scrawny chest, yelling, "Bullshit. You just want to wuss out, go home to Mommy." He howled like a baby and turned away.

"They never tell us anything and we've been here long enough." Emil addressed Udo's back. "Maybe they're afraid to tell us we lost."

Udo swiveled back and kicked Emil in the right ankle. It was a nasty quick move and Emil sucked in breath, but still managed to produce a heartfelt, "asshole."

Emil was ten inches shorter than Udo and would likely lose a fight, so I was glad Udo moved on to his next target, Otto, who was sitting red-faced and out-of-breath on a rock, massaging his neck.

When Udo mocked Otto, "How're you going to hold up as a soldier, when you can't even run a mile?" I tuned out, ignoring the questioning whispers in the back of my mind.

Emil sometimes mumbled about us walking home, but the subject never got much farther—just the thought of taking off alone on an unknown road without decent provisions made us stop in our tracks.

Since we arrived almost two years ago, our numbers had shrunk by a third to less than forty. In some cases, boys had been picked up by their parents, sometimes they were shipped back. These were the undesirables—boys with problems—bed-wetters and criers, and those who didn't keep up with our physical activities or fell ill with diseases. Why Otto was still here, I didn't know. He'd lost a lot of weight and his clothes hung on him like on a scarecrow. His sternum was concave and formed an oval divet on his chest, another reason we teased him.

Classroom instruction seemed no longer a priority.

After Wagner had left last year, we found out that he'd been drafted. In his place Herr Braun had taken over, his name a perfect match to the brown Nazi uniform he loved to wear. He was a retired SS military instructor and relished discipline like others enjoyed holidays, even outshining Steinmann. What he lacked in subject knowledge, he made up for in drills and punishment.

It started with saluting the flag at seven o'clock sharp. We marched to the pole and one of us, usually Udo, Braun's favorite pupil, stepped to the flagpole while the rest of us took position in a rectangular shape around him. Braun watched every move, made sure we stood straight, arms outstretched in Hitler greeting, eyes hypnotically watching the flag inching toward heaven.

If one of us wasn't standing perfectly or our increasingly tight Hitler youth uniforms lacked something, Braun zoomed in faster than an eagle swoops in on its prey. He'd squint, one eye hidden behind a black patch, a war injury he proclaimed he was proud of. "Shrapnel," he'd say, nodding to himself, "an honor."

Rumor had it, he'd caught more shrapnel in his bottom, but nobody was going to broach the subject. Supposedly, he'd spent months lying on his stomach while the doctors removed metal from his behind and sewed him back up. It was true, we hardly saw him sit and his walk appeared laborious at best. Maybe his injuries explained his sour moods and lack of patience.

Just this morning, Braun had singled out Otto because his closet wasn't perfect.

"What's this?" Braun's finger stabbed at the two orderly shirts and set of underwear. Somehow a ladybug had made it inside Otto's locker. Now it sat, unperturbed and minding its own business, on top of a grayish towel, its red wings and black dots gaudy against the drab fabric.

Otto squinted, his shortsighted gaze on the insect. "Don't know how it got there."

"You're supposed to keep your clothes spotless." While staring at Otto, Braun rocked back and forth on his feet, a tick he displayed when he was irritated. I doubt the ladybug had anything to do with Braun's anger.

Otto hung his head. They are spotless, I wanted to answer for him. Of course, none of us said a word, secretly glad Braun wasn't picking on us. At the same time I wished Otto could've gone home.

Instead of flicking away the ladybug, Braun's fleshy hand came down on Otto's towel and smashed the poor thing.

Somewhere near me Emil gasped. According to him ladybugs were harbingers of luck—killing one surely meant trouble.

"Clean it up, report to special training after lunch."

Special training meant strenuous marching or other senseless exercises. The worst was standing at attention for hours, holding a piece of tree limb as a makeshift rifle. If the unfortunate boy moved, Braun added more time. Head low, Otto carried his towel to the window. The way he walked he could've been at a funeral.

"I'm really tired of Braun," Emil said that same evening. "He torments Otto and looks at me like I'm some kind of criminal."

We were in the washroom where Emil scrutinized a new assembly of zits on his chin. I was giving myself a birdbath, craving the peacefulness of our bathroom at home. I could tell something was eating Emil, but he seemed nervous, his gaze wandering to the door every so often. For a moment it was quiet—with Emil you could be totally comfortable saying absolutely nothing.

When Emil remained silent, I quipped, "maybe that shrapnel will give Braun a hernia." I could tell something was eating my friend, but I wasn't going to press. The last thing any of us needed were nosy questions. Instead, I examined the frayed towel that had once been white.

I urgently needed new clothes too, especially underwear and socks. But my last two letters to Mother had remained unanswered. The dread animal inside me stirred and I quickly hung the towel to join the others.

No point worrying about home. Braun insisted the Führer was working hard to ensure our safety and that progress was being made all the time.

Did I believe it? Maybe.

If I'd taken time to sit back and think it through, I would've realized things were not as they seemed. Our meals had shrunk and were less varied. Lately, we mostly ate potatoes, the duty of peeling as constant as the itch on my scalp.

A month ago, lice had moved in and no matter how we washed, they refused to leave our skin and beds. During the day they weren't too bad, but at night I felt them roam through my hair. Imagining tiny feet climbing up and down to find a new spot to suck blood, my sleep was less than sound.

"Maybe we should offer to walk home on our own," Emil said, changing into his pajama pants. Like mine they ended above the ankles.

"Surely, we'd get a train."

"Maybe there aren't any." Emil's dark eyes were half closed in contemplation. His grandmother had been Hungarian, and Emil had inherited the eyes and dark skin from his mother's side of the family. Braun gave him threatening looks and talked about the importance of Arian blood and our German race. Emil didn't quite fit the picture of blue eyes and blond hair, and Braun had questioned Emil in detail about his heritage.

We heard plenty about dirty Jews who were stealing

from the country. I'd never met a Jew except for the owner of the local shoe store who'd gone away one day. Mother said he'd been sent to a labor camp, just like the communist family who'd lived at the corner of my street.

"I dreamed about cuckoos last night," Emil said. He'd worked his chin so hard, it glowed bright red. He had that look—his brows droopy, his mouth firm at the corners—but the real change was always in his body, which seemed to shrink as if it were pushed low under the burden of this new truth.

Of course, if I didn't ask, he'd bug me all night. "What does it mean?" I said.

Emil frowned. "Usually, if you dream about a cuckoo near your house, could be an owl too, there'll be somebody dying."

"Maybe at last Braun's shrapnel will do him in," I said with a grin.

But Emil remained glum. "Thing is, I saw swarms of them, thousands, like those murmurations of starlings, they all settled on our roof, until it was entirely covered, you know...in gray and white like striped cuckoo feathers."

The silly comment I wanted to make about Emil's fantasies stuck in my throat. All I did was nod and ignore the shiver creeping up my back.

APRIL 30, 1945

Monday after dinner we had shoe-cleaning duty. Polish was no longer available, so we used rags and spit, the leather of our shoes scuffed, the heels lopsided.

Even Udo's boots were in terrible shape though his father was some high-up official in the government. Tonight the mood was subdued. Dinner had been sparser than usual, last year's potato stores almost depleted. The weather continued to be unpredictable with sudden showers and freezing winds which didn't stop Steinmann from having us drill.

"How about we send postcards to our mothers and ask for care packets?" I said, using spittle to remove mud splashes. "They may get through easier than letters."

"I doubt Braun will allow it." Emil scanned the room to make sure our teacher was out of earshot. "Remember when Hans wrote something about the food portions? Braun made him rewrite everything, said it wasn't right to worry our mothers with trifle things."

"Since when is food trifling?"

Emil frowned. "I just can't help thinking that they're not

telling us everything."

Outside, a terrible noise rose—a roaring, grinding of wheels and screeching brakes.

In a flash we were all at the windows.

"What is going on?" Braun shouted somewhere in back and then pushed his way past us. I couldn't answer because I was equally fascinated and alarmed, my gaze locked on the beige tanks taking position in the yard.

"American Army," Emil cried.

"Lots of them," Udo added.

"They're going to kill us." Hans's eyes were wide with excitement and a pinch of uncertainty as he swiveled toward Udo. "We must fight them."

How, I wanted to ask. Tall, broad-shouldered men in formidable uniforms climbed from jeeps and trucks. Carrying machine guns, tank barrels directed toward us, they marched confidently toward the building.

"What do they want?" Braun huffed. He seemed flustered, and his authority he'd so generously used on us fizzled.

Looking shaken, he hurried toward the door, when Hitler Youth leader Steinmann rushed in. "Did you see? What do they want, what are we going to do?"

Braun seemed to regain some of his strength and rocked back and forth on his feet. "We will face the enemy." He turned to us. "Boys, follow me—"

The door tore open and banged against the wall as three GIs, machine guns aimed at us, marched in.

"Who is in charge?" asked the man in front in rough German. He was tall, the temples of his one-inch hair graying. Compared to us in our worn uniforms, he looked fashionable. Even the creases of his shirt seemed freshly ironed.

"Lieutenant Alfred Braun, sir." Braun puffed himself up

but still managed to look puny in comparison.

"Camp leader Steinmann in charge of management."

"Your camp is dissolved," the soldier said. "We're taking over."

"What do you mean?" Braun said, the last of his authority evaporated.

"German troops are defeated, we're assuming control over the area."

I stared at the American, then at Braun and the camp leader who seemed to shrink before our eyes. The GI's words reverberated through my head…defeated…assuming control. What did it mean? I recognized fear in Braun's eyes, yet all I felt was confusion. The American didn't move a muscle. "Hand over your weapons."

Steinmann looked at Braun and back at the American. "None here."

"Then you won't object to an inspection." The soldier didn't wait for an answer and waved at his men. Within minutes the building swarmed with Americans opening lockers and cupboards, picking through our meager stores and turning over our beds.

"Your country kaput," he said. "The Red Army is north, French and British troops are assembling in the west. Your Führer is finished." He slid a forefinger across his throat, his eyes hard.

As the word kaput rang in my ears, I looked from the soldier to Braun and Steinmann. What was he talking about?

Obviously, I wasn't the only one confused, because several of the boys started murmuring… But before we could ask anything, the American waved his machine gun. "You two, come with me."

Braun had gone pale and nodded, his black eye patch hanging crooked. He trailed Steinmann out of the room.

When Udo wanted to follow, one of the Americans stepped into his way, setting his legs wide. "You stay!"

So we all somehow made it back to our seats. I sagged down, my legs sort of weak and my mind a huge question mark. While we had been in camp, Germany had lost the war. No wonder our letters hadn't gone through. What was going on with Mother? Was she even safe?

At that moment, I realized I knew nothing about the condition of my country. And worse, I knew nothing about my family. Had there not been the soldier with his gun, I would've run upstairs to pack my bag. I needed to get home. Now.

"You think they'll kill us?" Emil asked quietly.

I shrugged. The schoolyard was filled with trucks, tank barrels threatening. A few shots and we'd all be gone. But somehow I didn't think these well-dressed and surprisingly polite soldiers would murder us. "Maybe we'll be arrested."

Emil shifted uncomfortably in his seat. "For what?"

For what, indeed? Being German, practicing war games? Believing in a great Germany and the Führer? Where was he anyway? And why had nobody told us anything? I should've been afraid, but the heat rising from my belly to my throat was fury. They'd treated us like imbeciles and we...I had believed everything.

I hoped Braun would reappear so we could ask questions, but he didn't come back. At some point we saw him and Steinmann, accompanied by two guards, cross the yard and disappear in one of the trucks. Still, we just sat there and watched from our seats while the American stood in the door like a beige statue.

Finally, Emil leaned over to me. "Where are they going?"

I kept my gaze on the man in the door, who suddenly straightened his shoulders and snapped a hand to his temple in greeting.

The original two soldiers appeared in the classroom and took position in front, followed by a man in an officer uniform. All four looked at us a bit like you'd look at lab animals before you do experiments.

"I'm Captain Jennings. Get your things and come with us," the officer said in surprisingly good German. He was lean and seemed very fit, although he had to be in his forties.

"What's going to happen?" Udo asked.

For a moment, the classroom sank into silence as if the American couldn't decide what to say. He just stood there and pressed his lips together, his stare impenetrable. "You'll see."

"We want to go home," Hans said.

"You come with us." This time the officer's voice was threatening, his narrow lips so thin, they disappeared. The guards' hands on the machine guns tightened a bit. If they wanted to harm us, they could. We owned nothing but a few sticks and the occasional pocketknife, used for playing silly war games. All of a sudden, I wanted to rid myself of the Hitler youth uniform I'd worn so many years. With pride, I might say. Not now, though. Now, more than ever, I wanted to go home to my mother.

Had I known what was coming I might have simply run outside and provoked them to shoot me.

APRIL 30, 1945 - EVENING

One by one, we climbed into tarp-covered trucks and sat down on long benches. There was no sign of Braun or Steinmann. None of us spoke.

I don't remember how long we rode, but at some point, through the fluttering canvas in back, I caught glimpses of the road that ran straight along railroad tracks. There was no traffic, not even a single person in sight.

"Maybe they'll take us to the station to go home," Emil whispered into my ear. Hope swung in his voice.

"Maybe." Somehow I didn't think the grave Americans were simply sending us home.

"I can't believe the war is over." Udo sat across from me, his shoulders slumped forward. He'd shrunk in the last few hours.

Deep down, I was relieved, but this new truth carried an ominous weight of its own. If Germany had lost the war, what did it mean for us? Would they put us in a labor camp or throw us in jail as prisoners of war?

The truck slowed. And something else registered—a terrible stench of a kind I had never encountered.

It settled on my tongue like a blanket of fussy mold, putrid and so strong, I wanted to wash out my mouth and bury my nose in my shirt.

"Look." Otto pointed outside. He sat closest to the back flap of the truck and since he hardly ever spoke, it was as if he'd screamed. Emil and I sat next to him and leaned toward the opening. To the left of the road, a gravel embankment rose several feet to a rail line.

On it bodies in gray or striped clothes lay strewn as if somebody had sprinkled them there at random. Some stared, some lay facedown, sideways—all of them had two things in common: they were thin as twigs, and they were dead.

As if my eyes had a mind of their own, my gaze wandered upward to the tracks, where a cargo train with open flatcars and boxcars stood motionless. Its doors were open and from my vantage point on top of the truck platform, I had an unhindered view of the inside. Each train car contained dozens more dead bodies. They stared with unseeing eyes, their cheekbones so pronounced, they looked like skulls with a bit of skin drawn across.

A shriek rose and I realized it had come from my throat.

"What is it?" Udo asked. Emil and I exchanged a glance. It was all I could do—breathe the stench and swallow, try getting the taste of death off my tongue without puking.

When neither of us said anything, Udo rose from the seat to peek outside. A frown spread over his face. I don't know what he had expected, maybe some kind of battlefield with a bunch of heroic flags raised to half-mast.

"They're all dead," he mumbled as he slumped back down and several others crowded to the back to peek outside.

More boys rose to look, sat back down, voices mingled, some higher than usual, some shaky with dread…"Did they get shot?...There are so many...Who are they?"

The rumbling of the truck stopped. I carefully looked around at my classmates, the guys I'd spent nearly every minute of every day with for the past two years. Heavy silence filled the platform. Emil's leg next to mine trembled. Udo still had that expression of shock on his face, a sort of wide-eyed stare. Otto, next to me on the other side, was quietly crying.

Against my will, I looked out again. Behind our truck more than thirty-five railcars stretched as far as the eye could see. The bodies on the embankment just lay there, tossed away and forgotten. Nearest to us, a young woman not much older than us lay on her side. She must've once been beautiful, even with the shaved head and that ghostly pallor. Her eyes were large and dark, framed by long lashes and perfectly shaped eyebrows. I stared into those eyes, willing them to blink and come back to life.

You know how certain moments etch themselves into our memories. It happens without knowledge or effort, a secret message our brain sends to the subconscious to never forget. This was such a moment, though at the time I didn't know it. For the rest of my life, I would see those dead eyes in the bony skulls staring into the darkening sky.

Questions raced through my mind. Who were those people? Why were they so thin, and why were they all dead? I would've understood dying in battle. This scene did not fit anything I knew about the war.

The truck's engine fired and we were moving again. The train ended and we passed through a huge cast-iron gate. I made out walls and barbwire...then a huge, squarish watchtower.

"They're putting us in a prisoner of war camp," Emil said, his voice hollow.

"But we aren't soldiers." Udo who'd been eager to

battle just hours ago, had a worry frown between his brows. "We never fought in the war."

"We wear Hitler youth uniforms and practiced," I said. "Maybe that's enough for the Americans."

The cloaking stench of decomposition grew stronger as we passed through another gate crafted from cast-iron ringed by a huge building. "*Arbeit macht frei*," it said above. Work frees you.

"What is this place?" Emil looked over my shoulder.

The truck stopped abruptly and the now familiar face of the guard appeared. "Out, make it quick."

We scrambled from the truck bed and assembled in a disorderly clump of thirty-some confused fifteen-year-old boys. Where was our marching training, our snappy salutes? Captain Jennings, the officer with the tight lips, appeared before us.

"Listen up," he said, pushing the cap back and then rubbing his own chin. For a second it looked as if he needed to clear his throat.

"Time to face what your Führer did to your fellow men." He paused as his gaze traveled past us. It wasn't a kind one; rather, it felt like a slap in the face with an icepick. "This is the concentration camp Dachau. While you," he poked a forefinger at us, "were playing your little games, thousands were dying here." He abruptly waved his arms. "Take a good look around, boys, because you'll be here for a while."

In the waning light stretched a huge open area and the path beyond, near endless rows of barracks on each side. But my attention was drawn to a second line of boxcars parked alongside, its floors caked with human excrement. Inside, men in US uniforms lifted and carried corpses, dead bodies so emaciated, they were no more than bones covered in skin. Some had bullet holes in their skulls, others had bruised throats or showed signs of force. Most were naked.

I abruptly bent low and heaved. Since I hadn't eaten in a while, bile dribbled into the dirt. A gust of wind carried the horrific stench and I heaved anew. My stomach wanted to turn itself inside out. All these people had died. Why?

Several of my classmates were also throwing up, the sound of retching and coughing in my ears. Out of a building on the other side stumbled several women, hats askew, and handkerchiefs in front of their mouths.

"Welcome to hell, *meine Herren*," Captain Jennings said. "This is your Führer's doing, called a death camp. Your little holiday away from home is over. Time to face your country's evil. Those dead men over there came from the concentration camp Theresienstadt to be burned here. Your Reich intended to hide its dirty work.

"Where, you might ask? This place is equipped with furnaces. Not for keeping warm in the winter, but ones to burn people...your fellow men were incinerated." The officer's voice cut like glass shards. "Oh, I forgot," he mocked, "you didn't call them people, they were *Untermenschen*...less than human, despicable Jews and Poles and Gypsies. Isn't that right?"

None of us made a sound and behind me rose the whimpering of an American soldier who stood near the cargo train and wiped his nose. I looked back and forth between the officer, the crying soldier and my classmates. Nothing made sense. Despite the cool evening air, I felt sweat run down my temples. It tickled, yet I was unable to raise my arm, not even my hand. My entire body seemed frozen with this new truth.

The officer stepped in front of Udo and yelled, "Isn't that right?"

Udo, usually so confident, stuttered something unintelligible and looked down.

"Well, times have changed and you are about to begin a new chapter." Jennings waved at another guard and spoke to him in rapid English. Then he turned on his heels, but not before throwing us the most hateful look.

"Come with me," the guard said, and so we staggered after him, a bunch of bedraggled boys who hadn't known a thing about our country or the war. I realized that even our teacher, the serious but generally nice Herr Wagner had lied to us. He'd supported our belief that the war was going well. Had he known about this camp? How could that word mean something so different?

In that moment, darkness descended and wanted to swallow me. Maybe I swayed or stumbled, but I felt a firm grip on my forearm. Emil's dark eyes bored into mine, and I don't think I had ever seen them so sad. We marched past rows and rows of barracks, each a hundred yards long, toward the back end. Here and there I registered men...on the path, between buildings. But I couldn't look at them, couldn't muster the strength to lift my head.

We entered one of the barracks. Just the smell inside made me want to run. It was different than outside, but no less potent.

The place was empty except for wooden partitions and platforms that reminded me of coffins.

"Find a bed, you'll be sleeping in here." The guard turned and left, and for the first time since the longest evening of my life began, we were alone. We looked at each other, the claustrophobic bunks, and the filthy bare floors. Tears glinted in Udo's eyes, something I would've thought impossible just hours ago. The boys we'd been earlier had vanished, only to be replaced... by what, though, I wasn't sure. Heaviness hung above us like weights we couldn't lift. The world we had known and thought we understood was a lie. All of it.

This new truth was too large to put into words, and for a while we just stood there, arms hanging, our gaze erratic and unseeing.

At some point joyous voices outside jolted me awake—I grew aware of my surroundings again. What could possibly be cause for happiness? One by one, we filed back outside. Hundreds of men in striped and grayish clothes surrounded a dozen GIs who were handing out packages. The striped men wore masks—at least that's what it seemed like because their faces were just skulls, their cheekbones so sharp, the bone beneath appeared to be poking through. Above shone eyes, tear-filled and impossibly large, the kind of eyes I'd never seen before.

"Thank you," they cried. "You saved us...God bless you." They reached toward the well-fed American soldiers, petted their arms and hands. Some of the tough GIs were crying as well as they handed out food and mess kits.

My own eyes filled with tears, and I turned away. Had the ground opened at that moment, I would've gladly jumped into the hole.

"What did they do to these people?" Emil said quietly. He was so pale, he looked as if he were about to faint.

I shook my head, my throat too thick to form words. They—the German government, Hitler, Goebbels, Himmler, all those men, the SS and Gestapo—had created a monstrous country. They'd started a war that sent millions of people away, my father, who I believed to be in France, among them. Was he in such a camp?

One by one, we returned inside.

"What do they want with us?" Udo said, traces of tears still visible on his cheeks.

"Maybe we have to bury...them." Emil had his gaze on one of the bunks. They were made of coarse wood and hardly taller than a person's body, more like drawers—

three coffins that fit above each other.

"You think they'll feed us?" Hans asked. He was short and used to be pudgy. Not anymore, though his face was still round as a soccer ball. Most of the time Hans was concerned with the next meal, though how he could feel hungry in this stinking room, with the terrible situation outside, puzzled me.

And how could we demand food when there were skeletons walking the camp—men who hadn't eaten well in years? Guilt washed over me as I realized the rumblings of hunger. I had no business to feel that way, no business to ask for food. These men outside needed to eat way more than we did.

"We could ask a guard," Udo offered.

"Let's wait a bit," Emil said. "They're feeding the starved men."

"I'm hungry," Hans whined.

"Maybe we should clean house," I suggested. "If we have to stay here, we better make it comfortable."

But there wasn't anything to do except to open the few windows. In a corner we found a pile of rags, grayish stinking piles of fabric that needed to be burned. There were no blankets, no brooms or buckets to clean with— nothing but wooden boxes for live corpses.

I sank on the floor and rubbed my forehead. In KLV camp we'd complained about our quarters, had squabbled about meals and the state of our beds. Now I knew that place had been luxury, a haven.

Outside it grew dark. When nobody showed up, we crawled into our bunks, covering ourselves with a few pieces of extra clothing, we'd brought in our suitcases.

Emil's cuckoo dream had come true.

May 1, 1945 - EARLY

I can't remember if I slept that night because every time I closed my eyes, I saw corpses...and the young woman's still face. I had the top bunk, Emil and Otto below me, so I stared into the darkness. Somebody had scratched a heart and the name Anna into the wooden rafter above. Below me, Emil and Otto shifted their weights, an occasional creak that told me they were awake as well. Somewhere in the distance, muffled cries sounded. I had no tears, no liquid inside me to produce them.

Had it not been for the growling in my stomach in the morning, I would've remained in my bunk. But just the thought of spending more time in here made me want to scream. I got up slowly because already I felt like an old man, my bones heavy and slow, my muscles withered, with nothing to look forward to other than finding peace in a grave.

"Out!" the guard from last night stood in the doorway, his eyes hidden behind gold-rimmed sunglasses.

As soon as we scrambled outside, an American, carrying a roundish canister with a long spout over his shoulder, entered the barracks. As he turned a crank, a white powdery substance fogged the air. The man walked around each bunk and methodically coated everything.

"Line up, spread your arms and legs, close your eyes," the guard outside instructed as soon as the American with the white powder was back. "It's DDT—kills lice."

Moments later, we all looked like bakers who'd rolled in flour. We shook ourselves and wiped the powder from our faces, trying not to get it into our eyes—not an easy task without decent towels and water.

The guard looked at us coolly. "Now come with me."

"Maybe we'll finally get some food," Hans said as we filed in behind the soldier. The striped pajama men were sitting in various spots in front of their barracks eating and drinking. There were thousands of them, but they hardly looked up as we marched past. I felt my cheeks burn, not because I envied them their meals, but because I felt such shame. These men had almost died from starvation; maybe they still would.

No, I could not eat, not like this. My insides were filled with some sort of gelatin, soft and wobbly and sloshing. Even my head felt that way, a dreamlike state I could not penetrate with logical thought. I moved my fingers, made fists. My scalp itched, and I thought longingly of the sweet-smelling soap in my mother's bathroom.

In front of a building, piles and piles of clothes and shoes lay in a heap: little shoes, large shoes, baby shoes, black leather shoes and women's heels. Somehow I knew that the owners of those items were dead.

The road went straight past twenty or so barracks. At some point we turned and marched past a group of ex-prisoners lingering on an open field. These men looked better, not as skinny, but still wearing striped or grayish outfits like oversized pajamas. I felt their eyes on us, heard

Udo mumble something to Hans, but could not make myself look up. Dust rose from the road and mixed with the stench in the air.

Near a guard tower lay corpses in German uniforms. From a distance they were nothing but gray ragdolls. "SS-men," the American guard shouted as he nodded toward the dead.

Years ago, I'd seen the SS arrest one of my neighbors, and I'd been afraid of them ever since. Here, they'd obviously run the camp, killed people by the thousands...my thoughts galloped forward. How many of these camps were there? Did I dare ask?

Emil let out a grunt, and when I looked over, I saw he was about to kick one of the dead men. "Assholes, damn swine," he hissed.

I put an arm around his shoulder, thinking that was going to calm him, but he yanked himself free and began shouting insults, the likes of which I'd never heard.

Terrified, the guard would punish him, I tried again, "Emil, please stop. They're already dead. What's gotten into you?"

Emil only shook his head, but finally seemed to calm down. I threw him a curious look, but he just stared at the ground, chewing his lower lip so violently, it began to bleed.

To my surprise, the guard didn't comment, but waved us to follow him to a brick building with a huge chimney.

"In here," he commanded, nodding toward a door with the title *Brausebad*...shower bath? Were we going to clean up now?

As we stumbled inside, my gaze lodged on four oversized brick ovens.

"You know what that was for?" The American shouted, his voice a hard echo from the bare walls.

We looked at each other as the answer crept into my

mind. They'd told us last night that people were burned here. This was a crematorium. And by the size of it, it was able to incinerate and destroy humans by the thousands.

"Yeah, that's right, take a good look." The American sneered now, his eyes wandering between the gruesome ovens and us. "Your Hitler and his men killed people and burned them here." He caught his breath and scoffed. "And that shower room over there, that was installed to gas people."

"But why?" Udo's voice was no longer boisterous, but small like a mouse.

The American shrugged. "I suppose to hide the evidence and make room quickly...for more murders."

Two more American soldiers appeared and hurried straight over to us. They spoke quickly, one of them waving his arms before pointing at us. A slow grin appeared on the soldier's face. In fact, all of them grinned—not easy smiles, but ones of malice.

"We've got news from your Führer," the soldier said. "He's had enough and killed himself."

I hardly heard the men's laughter; I was too busy trying to comprehend the news. Hitler's radio announcement bounced through my mind, the one from last summer when some fellow named Graf von Stauffenberg had tried to kill the Führer with a bomb. We'd listened open-mouthed, hardly believing our ears as Steinmann angrily paced the floor of our classroom. Was this a similar situation? Was the Führer still alive?

"How do you know?" Udo asked.

The tall American focused on him, the smile on his features frozen. "It's been confirmed, your Führer is dead— likely killed himself...coward."

Udo's muffled cry rang out. Some of the other boys sucked in air, but most of us gaped speechlessly at the broad-shouldered, well-fed Americans. It occurred to me that I hadn't known a thing about the man who'd sent my father and my friends' fathers to war or what he was really up to. Had I been living a nightmare or experiencing some sick hallucination?

Just as before, my throat closed up and my lungs wanted to deflate as the reality of this place returned full force and I imagined corpses being taken in here to be burned. It was incredible, sick and what? I couldn't find the right words, not even in my head. The Führer had been a monster. And the men who worked for him here had done so willingly and openly? They were monsters as well. Sick bastards. A sound escaped me, but I didn't recognize it as my own. It was that of a wounded animal wanting to hide from its hunters.

My knees returned to their jellied state. I leaned back on the wall, but immediately recoiled. Emil seemed worse. He was staring at the ovens as if he'd been hypnotized.

To my great relief, the American waved us on and I welcomed the air outside, even if it was tainted with death.

"I can't stand this," I mumbled as we returned to our quarters. Emil didn't answer— didn't even seem to hear me. He kept his gaze on some unknown point in the distance, and he probably would've walked past our barracks, if I hadn't pulled his sleeve.

"What's the matter with you?" I hissed, eyeing the two Americans doling out stacks of packages—our breakfast. "We better eat something."

To my great relief, Emil came to and even produced a thin smile. Which left the question whether I should go inside, where it reeked of filth and latrines, or stay out here, where the air was a death cloud. All of a sudden, I couldn't take it any longer. I hung my head and ducked inside, crept into my bunk and curled into a ball. I didn't want my classmates to see my tears or desperation.

Everything I'd believed in—everything they'd told us during the years in the Hitler Youth—was wrong. We'd been told to sacrifice, to believe in honor and glory, to fight for a powerful Great Germany. What was all that but rhetoric, inspiring words with no meaning. They'd lied. Hitler had lied. Our teachers had lied. Knowingly or not, they'd kept us in the dark about the true state of the country.

A hand landed on my shoulder. "You all right?" Emil's voice was heavy.

I forced my rigid legs to move once more and crawled out of my bunk. Emil seemed back to his old self and waved a tin can. "It's pretty good."

I don't remember what I ate that morning, because what followed let me forget that I even had a stomach.

MAY 1, 1945 - LATER

At eight o'clock we assembled outside. The American guard called it work detail.

Lined up in rows of two, we marched past the other barracks, the fake showers and crematorium, back outside the barbwire. Braun would've been livid because our snappy form had been replaced by as sort of dreamy strolling. We trudged without saying a word, each of us in our own world.

At some point we arrived at a cemetery called Leitenberg. Flags marked a rectangular space on an open field where soldiers and a handful of stronger looking prisoners—by the sounds of it, Poles—were digging a humungous hole. They ignored us, and if they spoke, we didn't understand them.

It didn't require any imagination to know what the hole was for. Sure enough, other men arrived dragging horse drawn carts stacked six feet high with corpses. The workers had covered their faces with rags, but it was impossible to escape the stench and the clouds of bottle flies. In fact, every flying insect from a five-mile radius seemed to converge on the dead—and us.

As I dug, the blisters on my palms blew up and began to leak. I thought about the men and women laid to rest in this mass grave. Nobody knew their names, and yet at some point they'd been children and teens, then adults—people with hopes and dreams, people who loved their families. Maybe they'd run businesses or worked in an office. They'd raised families of their own until...

My eyes blurred as I thrust the shovel hard into the packed earth, almost welcoming the pain in my hands, my stiffening arms and back. I needed to suffer because I was here, alive.

Nearby, Otto was struggling. Every couple of minutes he stopped and wiped his face, where sweat, snot and tears mixed into a slimy mess. Off and on he whimpered, which elicited whistles and catcalls from the Poles.

When I couldn't stand it any longer, I moved to his side and handed him a handkerchief. It wasn't clean, but it was better than nothing and thankfully, my mother had supplied me with a decent stack.

"Wipe your face, man," I said quietly. "Let's get this done, so we can go home."

Otto swished the cloth over his face, his expression reflecting surprise and thankfulness. Then he nodded and attempted to hand me back my hanky, "Thanks."

"Keep it."

"Why are you helping that loser?" Udo panted as I grabbed my shovel. He was sweating profusely, his cheeks and forehead bright red.

I squinted at him. I'd always been afraid of Udo, but at that moment, for the first time, I saw him for what he was: a scared bully who got his strength from tormenting others. In the horror of this new truth, he seemed grotesque, so grotesque, I smiled. "Because we've got to stick together…help each other."

Udo grunted something I didn't understand, then resumed digging.

The rest of the afternoon, Otto kept quiet, once in a while drying his face and throwing a glance at me.

None of us spoke on the way back to the barracks. It wasn't just the horrible task; we were plain worn out. My hands thrummed with open sores, and my shoulders and back felt as if I'd swallowed a board. A part of me welcomed this pain. It was something, at least, to show my respect to the dead.

Of course, we'd heard about camps over the years…labor camps where people who'd committed crimes went for punishment. But how could so many people be criminals? Why had nobody fed them?

Emil plunked down on the ground next to me. "What do you think they'll do with us?"

I shrugged, the military fork in my hand painful because of the sores. We'd picked up mess kits and after standing in line for thirty minutes, each of us received U.S. Army rations of canned mystery meat, crackers, coffee, gum and chocolate.

Emil investigated the chocolate wrapper—Nestle milk chocolate, it said. "Mmmh, real chocolate." He tore open the paper and took a tiny bite, his gaze rapt. "I'd forgotten what it tasted like." Resolutely, he stuffed the little bar into his pocket. "For later," he mumbled. The old pinched look was back.

That's what it had come to—a bunch of boys who couldn't even enjoy a piece of chocolate. Not here. Not like this.

MAY 2, 1945

The next morning I considered bandaging my hands, but there was no suitable material. The skin on my palms had either been rubbed off or was covered with blood-filled blisters. Each knuckle complained. Just thinking about holding another shovel made me want to curl up in a hole. Yet, a voice in my head taunted me: *what a wimp you are for doing a little digging when there is so much more suffering here.* The former prisoners who were still in camp—and there were thousands—appeared so fragile, they seemed half a step away from death.

And so I pressed my lips together and followed my classmates to the graveyard.

May 3, 1945

By the third day, I could hardly hold on to the shovel. Palms and fingers were covered under bruises and bloody blisters. My lower back throbbed like that of an old man. In fact, I walked hunched over, which brought back memories of my grandfather who'd died when I was seven.

Still they were bringing corpses, and soon the hole we had dug filled up. We were about to begin another when Captain Jennings, who we'd met a hundred years ago in our youth camp, appeared. Some of the guards talked to him, their gaze wandering to us. Despite the sweat dripping from my armpits, I shivered with dread as I imagined them shooting us, so we could join the poor souls in the grave.

Instead, the officer stepped in front of us and grabbed Emil's hand, which looked like mine. Then he inspected Otto and me with pinched lips. Without uttering a word, he returned to the guards and spoke to them in rapid English. A flutter of hope rose from my chest—maybe they'd send us home now.

While we were taking a break eating crackers and cans of beans, one of the guards appeared next to us.

"Come with me," he said. Emil and I exchanged a glance. The way I could tell, it was only early afternoon, too early to return to camp.

The soldier led us to a water hose and ordered us to clean up. Short of towels, we stood around waiting for our skin to dry, my hands and wrists burning from the cold water. A man with a red cross on his shirt appeared and in surprisingly good German asked us to show him our battered hands. He poked and prodded a little, then nodded to himself before rushing off.

Over his shoulder, he called, "Report to me in an hour...the tent with the red cross."

Confused, we returned to our barracks.

"What do you think he wants?" asked Emil, thoughtfully regarding his abused skin.

"I suppose, we'll get some bandages," Otto said.

I brooded silently. In my mind, the dim eyes of the dead stared at me. There were so many...and they were so light. Incredibly light, like children. Most of them had been starved to death. We had stacked them in the mass graves, one over the next, stacked them like wood for a fireplace. I'd tried to place them carefully, but where was dignity when you shared graves with hundreds and nobody knew your name?

Otto was lying on his bunk, staring into space. When I stepped to the window to peak outside, he called to me. "Thanks for helping me," he said quietly. "Here." On his palm lay a two-inch cross, carved from a bit of oak on a string. "Made it myself. Maybe it'll protect you."

I wasn't particularly religious, but at that moment I was willing to try anything. I hung the cross around my neck and thanked him. "Why didn't you go home last year...you know, when some of the others left?"

Otto's eyes grew misty behind the glasses. "Would've

loved that." His chin quivered, but then he stuck it out. "My mom is sick, has been for years." He looked around to make sure nobody was paying attention, then whispered, "She's in an asylum."

"And your dad?"

Otto shrugged. "Left years ago, couldn't deal with my mom." He tipped a forefinger against his temple.

"Man, you've got it rough," I sighed, secretly vowing I'd never be nasty to Otto again. The scene in the kitchen returned, the moment I'd called Mother a coward, the way her eyes had glistened over, the hurt and disappointment that had deepened the lines around her mouth. "My mom, before I left, I..."

I wanted to tell Otto...couldn't. He had no mother, I had abused mine.

When I looked up, Otto studied me curiously. Yet, he didn't say a word. I was thankful for that.

"All right, listen up." The medical officer, who wore a half-inch buzz cut and whose fingernails were cut to the quick within a hair's breadth, squinted at us, hands behind his back, feet spread apart as if he were afraid to keel over. "Since you aren't much good at digging, Captain Jennings has decided to send you all to help me." He cleared his throat. "I'll explain a few things...and expect you to follow orders."

We boys said nothing, just stood there sort of numb and scared. A guard with a machine gun lingered near the tent, and while he didn't exactly look at us, I felt he wouldn't hesitate to shoot if I walked toward the gate. All the Americans had this presence to them, this alert and neat appearance. They knew why they were here...to free the oppressed from a terrible fate. That made them strong. We, on the other hand, had nothing but guilt to deal with. We hadn't done the starving or the killing, but we had lived not fifty kilometers from here. Worse, we'd been ignorant, outright stupid. And something else: we had no purpose. For years, we had been told to hurry up and grow old enough to become soldiers, all to help the Führer create a Great Germany. Right. Hitler had killed himself after the war was lost. Nobody had found it important to tell us and provide some direction how we should continue, nor did we have any idea about the state of the country.

Fury brewed inside me and I felt my fingers cramp into fists, followed by the immediate pain from the sores. I relaxed my hands and took a deep breath. The terrible stench that had cloaked us had lifted somewhat, but it was by no means gone.

Death stuck to us with every breath.

I thought of Mother, and in that instant, I wanted nothing more than to sink into her arms and forget, have her care for me, like she always had...without question. In the youth camp I'd been able to push the anxieties about her away most of the day, but here anxiety about her safety kept me in its cold embrace. What if she was gone like Emil's parents?

"...important to wash your hands before and after," the officer said. "Now pull up your sleeves. The shot will protect you against typhus."

What was he talking about?

But before I had time to ask Emil, the man indicated for us to stand in a line. Following Emil's example, I rolled up my sleeve. One by one, we received shots in the upper arm.

I had hardly rearranged my shirt, when we headed toward the drill field. Once again, the air grew thick. But this time it didn't smell of death—it reeked of disease.

We filed past a long metal basin with water spigots. The American separated us into five groups. My group with

Emil, Otto and Udo and a couple of other boys entered the first barracks. Unlike our place, this one was filled with cots. They stood so close, their occupants could've held hands with each other. I sucked in air and immediately regretted it, because the stench was so intense, it seemed to drill into my brain with sharpened iron screws. Despite the many people, it was eerily quiet. A couple of orderlies hurried back and forth, the forms on the beds lay still.

One of the orderlies, an American with a severe limp, came over and separated us. "Each of you take care of a section."

Take care how, I wanted to ask. But I couldn't speak, could hardly breathe. I didn't even want to look at the poor shapes, had no knowledge of medicine. The only bright spot was that my area was near the outer wall where several windows let in air.

The man near me lay on a crumpled sheet with his eyes closed. He was as thin as the corpses we'd buried, but for some unfathomable reason, he was still clinging to life.

Across several beds I saw Emil sink to his knees and take hold of a patient's hand. I returned my gaze to the man in front of me. Other than a few tufts of grayish hair, he was bald, his skin pulled across bony cheeks, with the large eyes characteristic of a human who'd hungered for a long time. I kneeled down and gripped the his fingers, which felt like heated dry twigs. He lay quietly, but when he felt my touch, his eyes blinked a few times and then remained open.

"Hallo," I whispered.

The wrinkly neck twisted my way. He didn't speak, just looked at me.

"I'm Arthur," I stammered. "Can I help you with anything?"

The man's Adam's apple quivered. It obviously took a lot of effort to speak. "Thirsty."

Nodding, I straightened hastily and headed toward the back wall, where various medical supplies had been set up. From the words typed on them, they belonged to the Americans.

"I need water," I blurted at the first soldier who crossed my path. With arms outstretched and a disgusted expression, he was carrying a pile of crumpled sheets that emanated a terrible stench.

"Hold on, let me take care of this."

As I stood there, I watched my classmates. Some kneeled next to beds, some stood or leaned, some were walking around. All of them looked like they'd been hit by lightning, a shocked, incredulous expression that extended to their forward-slumping shoulders.

That was the first time I thought about escape. Maybe I could sneak out at night and find a hole in the fence? Idiot, I told myself. This was a former prison camp. There were no holes, just gates and men with machine guns who wouldn't mind shooting Germans. And who could blame them? Germans had created this abomination, Germans had starved and killed thousands, if not millions. Who knew how many camps existed? It was hot and sticky in here, yet a chill settled in the pit of my stomach next to the nausea.

"What do you need?" The American had returned and eyed me impatiently.

"Water...and a cup. Maybe also a washcloth to cool the guy down. I think he has a fever."

The orderly scoffed. "They all have spotted fever, caused by lice that live in clothes."

"Is it...does it go away?" I mumbled.

"Some survive, many do not. They're too weak already, just don't have enough strength." Again, the man eyed me. "We don't have many supplies, the Germans, your people, didn't find it important to care for the sick. They like'em better dead."

"I…didn't know."

"Funny, how nobody knows anything."

I really didn't, I wanted to cry. But all I said was, "Can I get water and a cup?"

The American threw me a curious look and then asked me to follow him. We marched outside where he motioned me to wash my hands, then down the path until we reached another tent. This one was huge and open on both ends. Tables and benches had been set around the outside. Steam rose from a makeshift stove. The man handed me a stack of five oval aluminum cups.

"Hand those to your companions, use the tap water at the sink. As far as I know, it's clean."

The man on the bed lay as before. The skin on his throat was splotchy, maybe that was why they called it spotted fever. From what the American said, he expected those men to die.

Trying not to think about it, I folded the cloth I'd discovered on a shelf into a rectangle and poured water over it. Then I carefully placed it on the man's forehead.

A moan rose from the man's chest as his eyes fluttered open. "That feels nice."

"I've got water for you to drink."

Supporting the man's shoulder and neck, I helped him take a sip. The feverish heat pierced the skin on my lower arm and hand as if I had burned myself. The man's eyes closed as he licked his chapped and near bloodless lips. "I'm Daniel."

"Arthur." I turned the cloth, which already felt warm. I needed a bucket of cold water to make a difference. The pails standing beneath some of the beds were used for nasty things. "Will be right back."

Frustrated that the American was nowhere to be seen,

I rushed back outside, remembered the sink and washed my hands and lower arms. What were the chances I'd infect myself with lice? In our camp we'd had lice, scabies and bed bugs. Hopefully the DDT powder had done the trick.

The scabies had been there when we arrived and had taken over the beds. Soon after, the itching began, the mites digging beneath the skin and causing red rash. I'd had them on my belly and armpits, Emil on his crotch, particularly his balls.

Luckily, Wagner, our teacher, had organized a doctor from a nearby village, who'd prescribed Sulphur cream to treat us. Women from the village came to help wash every spec of cloth and bedding.

The bed bugs arrived later. No idea where they came from, but again we had to clean, wash and disinfect with some horrible powder.

But at least we hadn't fallen ill. Daniel and all the others here were so sick, they couldn't even sit up, let alone take a step.

Not knowing where to turn, I tried the mess tent. "Need a bucket for drinking water," I told the first guy I saw. He wore a white shirt, so I figured he was a cook.

"Don't have any," the American said. "Try the commissary." He pointed down the path. "On the other side of the fence, can't miss it."

The gate stood open, but as soon as I came within thirty feet, two guards waved me to a stop. "Where to?"

"I was sent to fetch buckets for drinking water," I announced, trying not to let the machine guns intimidate me.

"What for?" One of them said. He had the squarest chin, making his skull look almost rectangular.

"The sick room...I'm helping to take care of the sick men."

The Americans looked at each other. Then one waved his gun. "I'm going with you, don't make me shoot you."

"Where were you?" The American in charge of the hospital barracks stepped into my path.

I lifted the two buckets, I'd been allotted, which I'd filled with water. "Got clean water to cool them down."

The man squinted suspiciously. "You've got *ten* patients, not one. See to them."

Ten? How was I going to take care of ten men, when I had no clue what to do? After switching out Daniel's cooling cloth, I began making the rounds. The men in beds two, three and six were delirious with fever, incapable of speaking." I washed their faces and dampened their lips with a few drops.

The man in bed five was dead. I didn't immediately know it, but when he hadn't moved, I finally touched his neck. He was cool, almost normal and the reddish pallor from the spotted fever had been replaced with a sickly yellow. In a panic I rushed outside to wash my hands, then back in to look for the American orderly. Again, he was gone, so I visited bed seven.

The patient in it was awake and looked at me with huge eyes. "I'm afraid I made a mess," he said quietly, his accent Polish.

When I lifted the sheet a nauseating smell hit me. Please, not this. Already, I felt sick to my stomach. When had I last eaten? I didn't know, couldn't think about food without wanting to puke.

Helplessly, I looked around. I wasn't the only one dealing with a soiled bed. Otto had turned a man on his side and wiped at his back. Then he gagged and dived between the beds retching.

I swallowed as revulsion and nausea burned my throat.

Momentarily, I looked away...toward the exit, contemplated running. I saw myself racing past the guards, climbing a fence, heard shots and then...

Ever so slowly, my gaze returned to the poor wretch in the bed. What if it were my father lying in some far away hospital? Fighting down my disgust, I forced a thin smile. I needed soap and water, clean sheets and pajamas. "I'm going to find something to wash with," I said.

By the time I arrived at bed eight, several hours had passed. The man in bed nine was also near death, his face covered in splotchy, bruised-looking spots, his chest aflame with fever. I placed a cloth from the only remaining clean bucket on his forehead and turned to bed ten.

"You're working hard," the boy said. He wasn't much older than me, maybe seventeen. Like the others, he had the characteristic coloring of spotted fever, but he didn't seem as sick. "Where did you come from?"

"Americans picked us up from a KLV camp," I said, trying to assess the boy's ailments. "You got any pain?"

The boy shook his head. "Just hot and miserable."

"Why are you here?" I carefully wrung out the last clean rag and placed it on the boy's forehead. "You're German, right?"

The boy chuckled, but it sounded bitter. "Always thought so...my mother is Jewish. They picked her up last year while I was staying with Grandmother in the mountains. Not long after, the SS came..." The boy shuddered and took a ragged breath. "Grandmother is gone now, so is my mother. Soon, I'll join them." He moved his mouth into a grin, his eyes gloomy as desolate puddles of rain.

Nonsense, I wanted to shout. Don't be an idiot. You've got your life in front of you. But he was no idiot, not really. He was just a boy who'd had the wrong mother...in a country that had hated him and his family. Hitler had told us Jews were bad people—that they didn't deserve to own things, that they brought disease. But this kid looked like me. In fact, he could've been my older brother.

"Can I get you something to eat?" I asked.

He shook his head. "Not hungry."

"Anything else?"

He closed his eyes. "I'm going to sleep for a while."

I rinsed the cloth and replaced it on his head. Then I returned to bed one.

Bony fingers clamped around my wrist. "You need to take care of yourself," Daniel said. I nodded, my mind still on the other boy, who'd lost his mother and grandmother to the SS.

For the past year Mother's letters had been so sporadic and slow, it was hard to tell what went on. Not once did she mention our fight, the nasty things I'd said to her. Now, I sat inside a camp with absolutely no news. I couldn't write, and Mother didn't know where I was. Was she wondering why I wasn't coming home?

A noise escape my throat, the hot twigs on my wrist loosened. "Sorry, I didn't mean to scare you."

"You didn't, I just...thought about my mother."

The man nodded. "I have not seen my wife or son in four years." Again, I stared, the words stuck inside me. "We were picked up together, but then they separated the men from the mothers. My son was only six..." A tear blinked in the man's right eye. "I miss them."

In an instant my throat closed up, tears pressed. What senseless misery.

Was that the first time my soul went flying, that tiny part of me that could not be touched? I imagined it taking off, flying away up into the clouds so it could not be touched and soiled by my body and mind and the unspeakable things

I saw and did.

All afternoon I rushed back and forth between the beds. At some point two men appeared and carried away the dead man in bed five. The same men appeared a few dozen times that afternoon. Others carried in new patients...the beds refilled in an unending stream.

I was just feeding the boy in bed ten some water, when Emil appeared next to me.

"We can go to dinner," he said in a low voice. "See you outside."

I nodded but kept my gaze on the boy's lips in bed. When I adjusted his sheets, he asked, "Is that your friend?"

"His name is Emil, I'm Arthur."

"Gero."

I patted Gero's hand and straightened. "I'll be back later. Can I get you anything?"

The boy grinned. "A nice Sunday beef roast, dumplings in sauce and apple streusel cake." He drew in air as if he were smelling delicious cake baking. "Butter streusel, my grandmother's recipe."

I smiled back. "Let me see what I can find."

Outside Emil lingered near the sinks. I washed carefully and joined him. Only now did I notice the ache in my back. It was different from digging, but no less painful, a cutting pain that ran the length of my spine. But worse were the men I'd encountered, their suffering and my utter inability to help them.

"I can't stand the smell in there," Emil said as we walked back to our barracks.

"Putrid."

Emil sucked in air. "I don't know if I can do this."

I placed an arm around his shoulder. "We've got to. Maybe they'll let us go soon."

Emil stopped so abruptly, my arm slid off. "Last night, I

dreamed about cutting wood, lots of wood, an entire forest." His voice lowered. "There'll be many more dying."

I swallowed. I'd never given much credit to Emil's superstitions, but right now it seemed he was right every time. Maybe he'd inherited some talent from his mother. He'd told me she'd been able to foretell the future. Emil had once mentioned that she'd seen the war coming as clear as day. After that vision she became very afraid, then confused. She took her own life by jumping in front of a train.

"Maybe we can escape," I said not very convincingly.

Sure enough, Emil cried, "How? Have you seen those guards, the towers and fences? They'll shoot us—"

"Shh," I hurried and grabbed Emil's arm. "Let's go back to our barracks and talk there. You never know who is watching and listening here."

Emil pressed his lips together and followed me.

But after dinner we were so exhausted, we just passed out. No matter the stink and the drudgery, I couldn't muster one decent straight thought.

MAY 4, 1945

The next morning, the guard walked us back to the makeshift hospital. After washing hands, I hurried inside, anxious about what I'd find. A hush lay over the room as if the men were all asleep. Like yesterday, Daniel lay on his bed. He'd attempted to pee in a bottle hanging on the bedframe, but he'd obviously missed some. The puddle on the floor gave off a sickly stench. I hurried off in search of cleaning equipment. Supplies were so meager, we had to take turns using buckets and rags. There was little to clean with, no soap or disinfectant.

Another soldier had replaced the American from yesterday.

"We need more supplies," I said, when he appeared in the door of the storage room, where I'd just snagged the last bucket. "How are we supposed to help the sick, if we have nothing to work with?"

The man looked at me with furrowed brows. "No idea." He shrugged and left.

"Very helpful," I mumbled, when Emil came running into the room. He looked flustered, two red spots burned on his cheeks.

"Need bed linens and soap, lots of soap," he cried, eyeing the few cups, plates, a handful of boxes of bandages, tweezers and hot water bottles on the shelves. This morning there were no fresh sheets, no pajamas, no pillowcases or anything else usable.

"What happened?" I asked.

"Got a blowout." Panic stood in Emil's eyes as he pressed his fists against his head. "What am I supposed to do?"

"We need to talk to somebody," I said, hiding the bucket behind a shabby curtain. "Come with me."

Emil, obviously glad to leave the foul-smelling room, hurried after me. Outside, we washed as instructed and headed toward the gate.

"Where are we going?"

"The Army's supply tent."

Like yesterday, the guard stepped into my way. "Where to?"

"Need to speak to the officer."

"About?" the guard barked. At least that's what I thought he said because his German was lousy.

In that instant, the powerless anger that had brewed inside me demanded to be heard. "The men in there lie in their own shit," I yelled, "how are we supposed to help when we have nothing to work with? How can they get better?"

Behind me a voice said, "They won't."

I swiveled around on my heels and found myself face to face with Jennings, the captain who'd brought us here. He looked at us calmly. The fury I'd just felt seconds ago was gone, replaced by the low rumblings of dread.

"I suggest you return to your work."

"To do what?" I heard myself say.

"Care for the men."

"We need sheets and soap and…stuff," I yelled once more, my throat hoarse from the unaccustomed effort.

"I suggest you leave this instant," Jennings snapped, "before I have you arrested."

"Who cares," I mumbled.

"What was that?"

"Nothing!"

"Maybe I should have you executed," the man said calmly.

I felt Emil's hand on my forearm. "Come," he whispered. "We are going back now," he declared loudly. "He'll do his work.

"What's the matter with you?" he cried as soon as we were out of earshot. "He was about to kill you."

"Maybe that would've been better," I said, avoiding Emil's gaze.

"Bullshit." Something in Emil's voice made me look over, and to my surprise he was sobbing. Not loudly, in fact he made no sound at all. "I hate it when you talk this way." His whispers were laced with rage. "Like your life isn't worth anything. That's what they wanted us to believe, the stinking Führer, the SS."

"But what if it's all gone?" I said. "What about our mothers, your grandmother? Maybe they're long dead."

"You don't know that." Now Emil was shouting. "Quit talking like that."

Then he turned his back and left me standing there open-mouthed.

I don't remember how I returned to the sick room or what happened that day. The men in beds 7 and 8 died and were immediately replaced by new men who resembled the others. That day, my soul went flying again. It went into the forest where we had done our training hikes and exercises, then it zoomed all the way home to the woods where I'd gone hiking with my parents. Right now, it floated amongst wildflowers like poppies, daisies and primroses that dotted meadows and field edges.

"Why isn't there any medicine?" Otto asked that night. Tear lines streaked his freckles, but he seemed determined to scrape every morsel from his bowl.

"Arthur tried this morning," Emil said. "The captain almost shot him."

Calls came from various beds as my classmates curiously looked at me.

I said nothing—couldn't because I was still numb and also angry at Emil.

Otto's face appeared in my vision. "You all right?" He seemed completely oblivious to the fact that his cheeks had whitish specs where tears had dried. All I saw was concern for me. For the first time, I noticed his eyes were green.

"Fine." I crawled from the bunk and joined the others. Udo, Hans and another boy were pitching pebbles into a cup. Hans was one of the guys who'd been sent to help with laundry, a nasty job they performed outdoors in zinc tubs. His fingers were still shriveled and bright red from spending all day in cold water.

MAY 8, 1945

About midmorning a few days later, I was just helping Gero eat a bit of watery soup, screams and shouts erupted outside.

Then one of the Americans appeared at the door, yelling at the top of his lungs, "Germany has surrendered. The war is over."

Muffled cries and laughter rose here and there, though the majority of the men were too ill to hear or comprehend. Across the room, Otto, Emil and I nodded at each other. None of us smiled. Was it relief I felt?

"At last," Gero said quietly. His fever had risen, his cheeks and neck were flushed, his upper chest damp. He pushed away the soup bowl I was holding in front of him.

"Just a few more bites," I urged. "Come on, you've got something to celebrate." It was a dumb thing to say to a boy who'd lost everybody he'd loved and now lay dying, all thanks to Hitler and the many who'd helped him succeed. Was I part of that group? Had I ever really thought about why my neighbor, the communist, had disappeared? Had I asked my mother for details about the war?

Gero put a scorching hand—his palms were hard and callused from working in a gravel pit—on my wrist and attempted a smile. "At least the war is over and damn Hitler is dead. Maybe Germany has a chance now."

"What do you mean?" I asked, keenly aware of Gero's fingers burning my skin.

He grinned at me with feverish eyes. "Clean it up, make it better." He squeezed tighter. "Maybe they'll let you go home now."

"Maybe," I said. "Now eat." I tipped the soup-filled spoon against his lips and he swallowed dutifully. "Good, now one more."

"You're pretty bossy," Gero said.

"I'm going to get a lot more bossy, if you don't eat."

"I'm not hungry."

"You just forgot how to be hungry. It'll come back to you. Now swallow."

Gero did and the bowl slowly emptied. Exhausted, he fell back on his pillow.

"Why are you making such a fuss?"

"Because you're not going to croak."

A chuckle rose from Gero's chest, followed by coughing. "Have you looked around?"

"So what," I said way too loud. "Just because others die, doesn't mean you'll have to." I leaned closer. "I asked the American medic, he said, only forty percent typically die. So, you better listen." I forced a smile, hiding the uncertainty and anguish I felt.

Gero closed his eyes. "Fine then, I'll work on it."

I placed new cooling cloths on his forehead and wrapped two more around his lower legs. Only when he fell asleep did I move on. Damn sickness.

MAY 12, 1945

It's true I spent more time with Gero than with some of the others. By the time many of the men arrived, they were already so weak, they had little chance of recovering. At least we'd finally received additional sheets, cleaning supplies, disinfectant, and donations of pajamas, so it was easier to care for the men.

Every evening we lined up as usual to be counted and receive our rations. There was no mention of going home, not that day or the next. Once in a while we saw Captain Jennings hurry past, but none of us were brave enough to ask. Udo had quit talking altogether, not a single boisterous, loud and often annoying comment could be heard. He didn't even bully Otto any longer, just sat quietly on the dirty floor every night or curled up in his bunk.

Each morning I rushed to sickbay. Daniel's condition worsened, no matter what I tried. He seemed to be comprised of bones and skin, yet he clung to life harder than some of my other patients.

"What are you going to do when you get out of here?" he asked me every time.

At first, I'd ignored his question. Then I got mad and told him I'd never leave.

"Nonsense," he said with that soft smile. "You will go home."

"How do you know?"

"Because it's the only thing that makes sense."

I squinted, suppressing the fresh anger. "I don't know what you mean. To the Americans we're nothing but dirty Nazis."

Daniel gripped my hand, his huge eyes hypnotic. "Don't you see. It has nothing to do with the Americans. It's all about you. His forefinger gently poked at my chest. In there, you carry hope. Nobody will take that away."

After that our game changed. He'd ask me what I was going to do when I got out and I'd tell him the most outrageous things.

"I'll Deepsea dive," I'd say. Or, "I will take my mother on a world cruise."

Together we'd laugh.

When I arrived one morning in mid-May, the sun outside shone warm like summer. The camp had thinned somewhat, those who could, had left. Others were waiting for a spot on a truck or train.

Daniel slept.

"Time for your birdbath," I said, placing a hand on his forehead. It was cool, too cool. Bending forward I already knew what I wanted to refuse to accept. He lay there still and peaceful, a peace I'd never been able to feel, had resented him for.

I understood he'd shown me humanity, had drawn from some unfathomable place in his heart to show me kindness and illuminate a path toward a life after camp—even if it was only in my mind.

All that without ever complaining. He should've been furious with me for getting away, for surviving what he could not. Heck, *I* was furious. I ran from the room, ran until a guard at the opposite end of the camp stopped me. I hadn't even seen him because I couldn't stop crying. All those wasted and destroyed lives, all that suffering. Against all odds, I'd hoped he'd survive, maybe go home to be united with his wife and son.

At that moment I knew I had to leave, because if I didn't, I'd die...maybe not of spotted fever or some other dreadful disease, but simply because I'd lose the will to continue. And so in my mind I began to envision escape, of seeing my mother.

Hope is a strange thing. No matter the darkness, it often appears when we least expect it. It's like this tiny flame after a long winter that refuses to extinguish no matter how cold and windy it gets.

"Where to?" the American guard asked. He wore full gear and carried an automatic rifle, which he kept pointed to the ground.

Surprised I looked up. "I...sorry, I can't...."

The guard stared at me. Did I imagine his expression softening? In the shade of his helmet, it was hard to tell what he was thinking. "Something I can do for you?" he asked.

I shook my head. "My...friend died," I stammered. Immediately, new tears burst and the guard grew blurry.

He nodded. "That's tough." Abruptly, he dug through his right pocket, fished out a Nestles chocolate bar and handed it to me. "Here." Behind me steps grew louder. "Better go now before you get me in trouble."

Managing a watery smile of thanks, I snatched the chocolate and walked off, head low, uncertain where to turn. Not fifty yards down the path, Jennings came my way.

Not wanting to be screamed at, I ducked right and hurried down a narrower path between two barracks, breathing a sigh of relief when the officer headed straight toward the guard.

A few weeks ago, I would've been delighted to eat chocolate, but now? Even though I noticed its flavor and sweetness, it felt wrong to enjoy something...anything.

Emil lingered near the sinks when I returned. "What happened?"

I knew my eyes gave me away, so I shrugged. "Daniel died." After his outburst we'd resumed our friendship though I often noticed his far away expression. But then, maybe I looked the same. None of us acted like we had just a few weeks ago.

"Who?"

"A man I was taking care of."

Emil placed a hand on my shoulder. "There are so many, I just can't..." He shook his head. I know, I wanted to say, but my throat was tight again.

Emil straightened and looked at me. "Maybe being shot isn't so bad."

"Quick, for sure."

We looked at each other. What had become of our sense of adventure, our zest to march into war and shoot Russians? What folly, what naiveté.

Inside, I rushed back to Gero's bed. He was awake, but his eyes looked feverish.

"Got a treat," I said, fishing the chocolate from my pocket.

"Didn't I just eat soup?"

"That was hours ago."

A sigh rose from Gero's chest. "Not hungry."

"Nonsense." I broke off a small piece and stuffed it between Gero's lips. "Here, try this."

His eyes opened a bit wider. "It's so sweet. How in the world did you get chocolate?"

"Better eat another."

"Only if you have some too."

So it came that Gero and I shared the chocolate bar. Afterwards, I made him drink a full cup of water.

MAY 20, 1945

When I returned from the hospital in the evening—I was late because I'd given Gero a wipe-down bath and made sure that he had plenty of water—shouts could be heard through the open door of our barracks.

Several guys crowded together. Only when I drew closer did I notice Udo in their midst. He was lying on the ground, hugging himself, whimpering and muttering.

"What's the matter with him?" I asked, searching for strength despite the woozy feeling in my head.

"I found him like this." A worry frown darkened Otto's freckled face. "Wouldn't say anything, wouldn't get up."

"We better get the medic," I said. "He may be sick."

"You want him to lie with the others...in that nasty hospital?" Hans's arms flailed as if they weren't attached.

"What if he has spotted fever?" I said.

Emil bent low to feel Udo's head. "No fever."

"Udo, can you hear me?" I asked, getting to my knees next to him. "Can you get up?"

Nothing. Udo kept staring and whimpering.

"What's wrong? We want to help you." I straightened

and addressed the others. "We should at least put him in his bunk."

While we were eating dinner, we watched Udo lie on his side. He had lost more weight, and the shirt he wore hung in loose folds around his chest.

In the middle of the night, he began to speak coherently—except he was having a conversation with his mother. It sounded so lively, you would've thought she was sitting by his bed. Of course, we only heard his side.

"...I'm going, even if you and dad are saying no.

"...of course, it's safe. Herr Wagner said so, better than staying here and waiting for British bombers.

"...I'd rather you didn't visit."

He laughed at something, an eerie sound in the darkness.

By morning, he was still asleep when we were getting ready for assembly. The Americans never missed roll call. He looked confused when Emil and Otto tapped him by the shoulder, then turned on his side and closed his eyes.

"Come on, Udo, let's go. We've got to line up," Emil said slowly as if he'd be speaking a four-year old. "You don't want to get arrested."

Again, Udo stared at us funny, but dragged himself from the bunk. Together, we marched outside, where I kept a firm hand on Udo's right shoulder so he wouldn't wander off.

"This isn't working," Emil whispered as the American guard perused his clipboard. Udo was trying to sit down, and we had to hold him straight.

"Something the matter?" the guard said.

"Nothing, sir," Emil said loudly.

"Pull yourself together," I hissed in Udo's ear. "They'll arrest you."

For a moment that seemed to work, and the guard

began to read our names.

"Hans Heiden," the guard read.

"Here," Hans yelled.

"Udo Bauer."

Udo was half leaning against Emil and didn't react. "Udo?" I whispered.

Nothing. Udo's gaze was unfocused and he tried to sit again.

"Come on," Emil hissed.

"Udo Bauer?"

"He's here," I cried just as Udo sagged to the ground.

The guard's clipboard sank as he yelled at another soldier to join him. Before we had time to get Udo up, the Americans were upon us.

"What's wrong with him?" the guard asked.

Nobody said anything as the two soldiers shouted at Udo, who looked confused and then decided to curl up on his side, arms covering his head as if he were afraid of being hit.

Hans stood next to him, his incredulous gaze fastened on his friend. "Come on," he cried, "be tough, man, what are you doing?"

"I think he's sick," I said, tipping a forefinger to my temple.

The second guard showed up and yanked Udo to his feet. Udo began shouting something unintelligible and swinging his fists at the man, who gripped him firmly by the upper arm and led him away.

"Back in line," the guard yelled. He seemed to have no patience.

In front of me, Emil's shoulders sagged as he rubbed his eyes. At first, I thought he was crying, but instead he sort of froze while watching the guard.

"What's going on?" I whispered.

Emil only shook his head.

One by one we were called, after which the guard marched off with his clipboard.

"What will they do to him?" Otto asked. "Should we ask the Captain?"

"Over my dead body," I said, trying to hide my shock. I'd never liked Udo—he was an idiot most of the time—but he'd been the strong one. Maybe that had been an act. "Jennings will just blame us."

"Maybe they'll take Udo to sickbay." Emil looked as worried as I'd ever seen him. It surprised me because he'd sometimes been on the receiving end of Udo's jabs.

But Udo wasn't there, not in our barracks nor the others. I made the rounds, hurrying from bed to bed, cleaning, cooling and wiping. Only at Gero's cot did I spend extra time, washing his face and chest and helping him eat a bit of oatmeal. His fever was lower this morning and he seemed more alert.

"Something bothering you?" he asked.

"One of my classmates went crazy and they took him away." I hesitated, but then told Gero about Udo's collapse. "He isn't one of my favorite people, but something is wrong and I'm worried—"

"Might me a nervous breakdown."

Our eyes met. "From the trauma, the many dead people?"

Gero shrugged. "Could be. He likely expected to win the war."

I must've made a face because Gero began to laugh. "I was right, hahaha."

I couldn't help but smile back because this time Gero's mirth was real. "He was totally into the Führer…"

"Thought so." There was the smile again. It made Gero look like an entirely different person—his eyes seemed to sparkle in the gloom, and the corners of his mouth twitched. Just as quickly, he was serious again, the old strain weighing down his features. "I better sleep some more."

I straightened his pillow. "You're doing better, you'll see."

Gero nodded with closed eyes. Only when I tiptoed away did I discover Emil leaning against the doorframe of the nearly empty storage room.

"Something the matter?" I asked, drawing near.

"You seem pretty chipper, considering what's going on."

"What do you mean?"

Emil furiously rubbed his nose, which looked inflamed as if he'd caught a nasty cold. "I've got to tell you something."

Oh no, not again, another prediction. "Let's walk then," I said reluctantly. By now the corpses had been buried and the air outside was a bit better. A watery sun peeked through the clouds as we washed. "What is it this time?"

Emil threw me a glance. "You think this is fun? Having these dreams and feeling things?" When I remained silent, he continued. "My nose began to itch as soon as they arrested Udo. He's going to die."

"The Americans are going to kill him?"

Emil shrugged. There were limits to his premonitions.

"I don't see how you'd know." I thought about the coocoos, the little voice in my head insisting that Emil *did* know.

"My mother could."

"Your mother?"

Emil nervously looked around and when he confirmed we were alone, he said quietly, "She was a gypsy. Well, we call ourselves Romani. Even as a girl, she saw things happen way before they did. She didn't commit suicide; she was taken by the SS, and my father was killed when he tried to stop them. She was likely in a camp like this one."

I stared at my friend, my mouth open.

"I was afraid to tell you," he said, his gaze contemplative. "They've got spies everywhere."

"You didn't think I'd snitch you to the SS?"

Emil slowly shook his head as his eyes found mine. "Not exactly, no, but Augustina made me swear never to speak about it. I...am sorry, I should've told you sooner. It's just...I can't lie anymore. Not to you." He waved his arms. "Not when all we lived were lies, even our KLV camp was nothing but a lie. Hitler was a mass murderer, those guards too. The entire country, the war...all lies."

I placed an arm on Emil's shoulder. What terrible anguish he'd encountered. "Maybe she's still alive," I said aloud.

Emil's eyes grew large. "Unlikely, as she was arrested years ago...before grandmother and I moved here." He chuckled, but it sounded bitter. "Augustina isn't my real grandmother. She was my parents' neighbor in Burgenland in Austria. Took me under her wing after her grandson died of meningitis. I took his place and we moved to Herten. My real name is Jani."

Emil couldn't even use his real name. No wonder he kicked those dead SS-men. "Hopefully, you won't have to hide ever again."

Emil scoffed. "I don't even know if Augustina is still alive."

The worry in Emil's voice mirrored my own. I gripped his forearm, Daniel's words in my mind. "Like you said, we've got hope. Let's not let ourselves be torn apart by anything."

He threw me a lopsided grin. "Maybe I was wrong."

"Nonsense." We'd reached the back gate when I noticed the same guard who'd given me chocolate. I waved at him and smiled before turning back to Emil. "Wait a second, I'll be right back."

"You feel better today?" the American asked when I approached.

"A little. Thanks again for the chocolate."

The man who had to be in his early twenties fished another candy bar from his pocket. "Here, I can't eat them all."

"How long will you be here?" I asked.

"Not sure; maybe until the camp dissolves, likely for years." He seemed to hesitate and then asked, "Who is your buddy?"

I turned around and waved Emil over. "My friend, Emil. I'm Arthur. You think they'll let us go home?"

The American drew another chocolate from his pocket and threw it to Emil. "Tom Williams." He scanned the road behind us and added, "You better go before I get in trouble. Jennings has eyes everywhere."

"He's nice," Emil said on the way back, unwrapping the chocolate. It was best to immediately eat because there seemed to be an abundance of bugs and vermin waiting for a snack. I knew somebody who needed the treat even more.

"Tell me about your mother," I said.

The clouds on Emil's face seemed to lift a bit as he began to speak. She'd been a beauty with thick raven hair and dark eyes, Emil's eyes, that could foresee the future. At least that part of Emil's story was true. After she met Emil's father at a dance, they'd settled on a small farm, where they'd raised chickens and kept a few pigs and cows.

"She had a beautiful voice," Emil said. "Often sang to me. That day, she'd promised to teach me the violin...as soon as I'd taken care of our cow. The old girl had wandered off and I went to find her. When I returned, my father lay dead in the yard and my mother was missing."

I imagined a younger Emil finding his father in a puddle of blood, then running through the house in search of his mother, losing both his parents in an instant, his life evaporated. I shivered. No wonder he was superstitious and looked for signs of doom everywhere. Well, he didn't have to look very far these days.

"My neighbor came running as soon as she saw me and hid me away. Her son had just died and she let me take his place."

"She saved you," I managed breathlessly.

Emil nodded. "What if she's dead?" He looked at me, his eyes large but dry.

"I bet she wonders why you aren't coming home."

I looked over my shoulder. Dozens of ex-prisoners were sitting in front of a barracks, but there was no sign of Americans. "Maybe we can escape."

"How? They've got the place surrounded. Barbwire and watchtowers everywhere. The death camp is turning into a prison."

"We could try to find some striped outfits."

Emil spit into the dust. "The Americans run a registry. Every person who leaves has to show a pass. They'll know from a mile away that we're not ex-prisoners."

Silence rose between us. Emil was right. We had to find another way.

MAY 25, 1945

By the last week of May we were still in camp. Fewer people were dying now, but there were still hundreds sick and too weak to leave.

The Americans had quarantined the camp because spotted fever and typhus hung around like flies persist near manure.

Udo was being held in a cell. Hans, Emil and I had visited him yesterday. He was calm and pretty much silent while the three of us told him of the ant races we held in the sand and Gero's continued recovery. It's true, I was a little proud of my care, but he was not out of the woods yet.

"He's a dirty Jew," Udo said.

I watched my classmate, a boy I'd been around for two years. He had to be blind and deaf to talk like that. "He's super nice," I said firmly. "A boy just like us."

But Udo didn't answer and I knew he was reciting Hitler talk in his head. I decided to let it go. "Can we get you anything?"

Udo curled up on his cot and turned his back to us. "Don't need anything."

"We'll ask the Captain to release you," Emil said as we left.

The next morning after breakfast, Emil and I went to speak to Captain Jennings. Rumor had it he was leaving soon, and sure enough he was carrying a green canvas bag to a jeep.

"Sir, may we speak to you?" I yelled while two guards immediately stepped into our way.

Jennings squinted and then recognized us. "Make it quick."

"We'd like to ask if you could have Udo released?"

Jennings' lips disappeared as he watched us thoughtfully.

"Your friend is dead. You would've heard soon anyway."

Emil and I looked at each other, then back at the captain. "You killed him?" I whispered, imagining how I'd wrestle away the man's holstered gun and use it on him.

"Nonsense! Took his own life...cut his wrists last night. Guards found him this morning."

In my mind I saw Udo showing off his pocketknife with the engraved swastika. It had been from his father. How he'd kept it hidden was a mystery. Once again, Emil had been right.

At times my soul stayed out a bit longer, sneaking back late when I was already in my bunk and asleep.

Today was such a day.

JUNE 1945

Every day during lunch break, I took a walk to the back gate where I spoke with the guard, Williams. I'd found out that he had a brother my age who attended tenth grade in Seattle. He still gave me chocolate on occasion, which I always carried back to Gero.

It was the one thing that made me happy. Gero was recovering. I gave him all the food I could scrounge and slowly, but surely, he grew stronger. His fever was about gone and together we began to walk, me holding him upright with one arm around his waist. After the long bed rest, he had to relearn to walk, his thighs as skinny as my calves.

"You're doing it," I exclaimed the first time we went outside.

Gero lifted his face to the sun. "Glorious."

After that it was a matter of time, our walks a little farther every day, our conversations circling around our past lives.

I took care not to become too close to the other men under my care. After Daniel's death it hurt too much to see them weaken and die. So I washed and fed them, cooled their burning foreheads and spoke to them about the weather and getting better.

At some point we were offered to switch to laundry duty, but I refused, wanting to remain near Gero.

And then one day toward the end of June, Gero was sitting on his bed in street clothes.

When he saw me, he waved, that tentative smile that so changed his features, on his lips.

"Leaving today," he cried, getting up.

So soon? I wanted to say, but all I did was hug him, carefully, because the boy inside those clothes seemed so fragile. "Glad to hear it," I said.

We'd discussed his leaving, returning to his home near Bremen, where he hoped to find remnants of his family.

"I'm catching a ride with an Army truck going north."

I pushed away my disappointment, having somehow imagined us leaving together, traveling together. *Selfish bastard*, I scolded myself. Be happy for him to get a ride. I *was* happy for him.

I accompanied Gero to the front gate, where several trucks lined up in a perfect row.

"Take care of yourself," I managed. "Promise to write when you settle. You know my address." We'd memorized each other's addresses, paper impossible to find.

Gero put his tiny bundle to the ground and pulled a leather cord over his head. I'd seen it many times during washing. "Here, for you, so that you find your way home soon."

At the end of the string hung a tiny compass, more like a toy than a real one.

"But it's yours," I cried.

"You saved me, gave me hope," Gero said. "Get out before this place swallows you." He placed the cord around my neck, next to Otto's string with the cross. "We'll meet again some day, you'll see."

The trucks revved their engines and pulled away, leaving me in a cloud of dust. The last thing I saw of Gero was his still bony hand, palm out in silent farewell.

JULY 1945

July was hot. And the hotter it grew, the more miserable I felt. The air was tainted with the stench of sweating and sick people, their excrements and filthy clothes. No matter how diligently we worked, men still died, though thankfully fewer now. They had closed the other six sick barracks and a number of cots sat empty. We also had a lot more supplies and were able to change sheets and clothes.

During breaks I dragged myself to a tree near the back gate where I sat and dozed. With Gero's departure, my energy level had dropped. We received rations as before, but the horrible suffering of so many people had drained me. Deep in thought, I held the compass in my hand, wondering if Gero had reached his home and found his family.

"How are you?"

Confused, I looked up and discovered the guard by the back gate. He'd installed an old umbrella to hide from the scorching sun.

I straightened, the muscles in my lower back seizing up with pain. Slowly, I ambled toward the man whose forehead glistened and whose beige uniform was dark with sweat.

"You okay?" he asked.

I shook my head. All of a sudden, despite the heat, I shivered. When was the last time somebody had asked me how I was? Not since Mother… Tears spilled as I remembered the week before I'd left for camp, our fight, me calling her a coward. She'd been so sad and worried. But I, the great idiot, had told her, it was my right to leave, that I was glad to get away. I remembered my enthusiasm, my excitement. My face burned with shame. If she was dead, I wouldn't even be able to explain anything. Hitler would've won, his betrayal—that of most of the adults I'd encountered—complete.

Oh, what I would've given to travel back in time and talk some sense into myself.

I thought about Udo who'd believed everything, had been the Reich's pawn. No wonder he killed himself.

I swallowed and cleared my throat. A blurry guard leaned his rifle against the fence and motioned me closer. Wiping my face with a sleeve, I approached.

"You okay?" he asked again. "Sorry, don't have chocolate, too hot right now."

I took in the sweat-stained shirt and reddened cheeks of the man. "Must be miserable, standing here all day."

"Pretty bad, but I'll be changing soon." He scanned the area carefully and returned his gaze to me. "Listen, you probably saw the extra troops and the barbwire. There're making this place into an internment camp, you know, for Nazis—a prison, only the other way around."

I remained silent, trying to comprehend what Williams was saying.

"I'll be a regular guard."

I stared at the man. "Good for you."

The American scoffed. "You don't understand. This

place will swarm with SS and Gestapo, all the scum from the bottom of our shoes, the kind your Hitler liked. You're so young, you should leave before it's too late."

How, I wanted to cry, but my face must've said it all.

The guard leaned closer. "I'll help you. Come back tomorrow morning, early. My shift starts at five. It's going to be dark, we'll talk then."

I nodded numbly, my soul returning early from its flight. I needed to tell Emil.

JULY 15, 1945

"How is he going to do that?" Emil asked. "What if they catch you?" We were sitting by ourselves outside in the waning light. None of us enjoyed sleeping in our bunks when it was so hot and the air cloaked us like a steamy, stinky blanket.

"All he has to do is let us out of the gate."

"Us?"

"You're coming with me." In that instant, fear squeezed my insides. What if Emil was afraid to go, what if the guard wouldn't allow it? I'd walk four hundred miles alone. I'd never make it.

A low chuckle rose, and Emil slapped my back. "Of course, I will. Can't let you run around like an idiot, likely get lost."

As I rubbed the tiny compass near my heart, relief flooded me. Emil was going with me, and we'd be able to tell direction.

I lay awake most of the night, afraid I'd miss the five o'clock meeting time. Otto still had a pocket watch he kept hanging by his bed. Every so often, I got up and crept, watch in hand to the door to catch the outside light that shone on the side of each barracks. At four thirty I decided to get up. I was about to hang the watch on the nail by Otto's bunk, when he gripped my hand. I was so surprised, I squeaked.

"What are you doing with my watch?" Otto asked, his eyes curious and a bit suspicious. In the shadowy light and without glasses, he looked like a ghost.

"Nn...othing."

Emil stirred, dark head of hair rising from the middle bunk. "Shh."

"Time," I said, trying to ignore Otto.

"For what?" Otto said way too loud.

Emil, who'd climbed from his bunk, hissed another "shh," and pulled me to the door.

"What if he tells the others?" I whispered.

Emil scanned the grounds outside and said, "Maybe we can leave tonight."

"Without our things?" It was true, we didn't have much, but I still owned a cardboard suitcase, I was planning to carry along. Inside were rather small pajamas, a threadbare towel, the remnants of Hemingway's For Whom the Bell Tolls, a gift from my father which I'd read a thousand times.

I was calculating in my head. "They may find us so close to morning roll call."

"Where are you going?" Otto's voice was unmistaken.

Damn, the guard would be angry if we showed up with three people—he'd only suggested helping me, not a bunch of guys whose absence would be noticed immediately.

I turned to face Otto, thinking of the cross he'd given me. "Listen, we've got to figure something out. At least do us the favor and wait here. I promise I'll tell you."

Otto nodded—at least I think he did. It was hard to tell in the low light inside the barracks.

Without another word Emil and I broke into a run.

Near the back gate, we slowed down. The guard stood quietly and I thought he may be sleeping, but when we drew closer, he called out, "Who goes there? This gate is closed."

I did a double take. This wasn't the voice of Williams, the friendly guard, who'd fed me chocolate for weeks. This guy sounded older and hostile at the same time.

"That him?" Emil murmured.

"Sorry, we got lost," I called to the guard and in Emil's ear, "Not him, we better go."

"Don't let it happen again," the American shouted after us, waving his rifle for emphasis as we scrambled out of sight.

"What's going on?" Otto emerged from the shadows. "Are you leaving?"

Again, I gripped Otto's shirt. "Listen, we may have a guard who can help, but if this gets around, we are all in trouble."

"I want to come with you." Dark spots burned on Otto's freckled cheeks, he blinked repeatedly.

"That's what I was afraid of," Emil said dryly.

"Please," Otto cried. "I can't go on like this. It's killing me, all those sick people. They're all dying and I just can't—"

"Shh!" Emil said.

I listened for sounds and when nothing moved, I said, "Let's go back to our bunks. We'll talk later."

But I couldn't fall back asleep—not now when my mind churned with questions...where was the guard? Had I misunderstood him? His German was lousy—maybe I'd gotten the time wrong? That had to be it. I'd try again later.

But what if he'd been transferred? Or somebody overheard him speak to us and he got punished? The thoughts wouldn't quit.

I was still awake when the morning siren rose. Tired and confused, I lined up outside, wishing once again I could somehow fly home…to my mother, my clean bathroom and hopefully, urgently, my father.

All morning while I took care of patients, I thought about what to do, rubbing furiously at the tiny compass hiding beneath my shirt. At lunchtime I grabbed Emil. Outside, American soldiers with machine guns at the ready marched alongside a group of men in tattered uniforms and civilian clothes—Germans. Somewhere, a voice shouted English commands. Williams had been right. The U.S. Army was filling the camp with Nazis.

I was about to comment to Emil when from the corner of my eye I noticed movement. One of the German prisoners was waving at us. He was filthy and covered in dust, his shirt torn, revealing reddish scars like large pockmarks.

Only when I zoomed in on the man's face did I recognize our old teacher, Braun. He'd lost his eye patch, the socket an empty scarred hole. It looked ghastly, but not as ghastly as the man's expression. Nothing was left of the arrogant short-tempered teacher. Instead, his demeanor exuded fear, his good eye blinking nervously as he tried for a smile. Even his wave seemed shaky and weak.

I gave a nod, unsure what I was supposed to do, and watched the prisoners disappear in one of the barracks toward the end of the main compound. These men had supported Hitler's regime, had been responsible for starving the people in here, killing them. They'd murdered Emil's and Gero's parents, and countless others.

I walked faster, Emil trying to keep pace. "Was that Braun?" he asked breathlessly.

"Hard to believe." I wasn't sure how I felt. I'd loathed Braun, feared him for his temper and cruelty, his unpredictable outbursts. Most of all, I hated how he'd tormented weaker boys like Otto or the numerous others who'd long since gone home. Yet, seeing him beaten down and stripped of his authority, I almost felt sorry for him. But then I remembered Emil. People like Braun had killed Emil's family, and I had no doubt Braun would've sent Emil to a concentration camp, had he known his true background. I set my mouth hard. "Maybe he gets what he deserves."

When the back gate came into view, the same guy was standing at his post, at least I assumed it was him. He was older and looked grumpy, squinting at us from a distance. This time we harmlessly walked past as if we were going to another barracks.

"How are we going to find the other guard?" Emil asked on the way back to the hospital.

"No idea." It was true, I was clueless. I only knew the man's name. Again, my fingers traveled beneath my shirt to Otto's cross and the compass. *It'll guide you*, Gero had said. *How?* I wanted to scream.

And then, in an instant, I knew what to do. "Go back," I said to Emil. "I've got to try something."

Ignoring Emil's curious expression, I rushed off. With every step I got more nervous. Two guards with machine guns secured the main administration building, the Americans were using as their office. Instead of slowing, I forced my legs forward. They couldn't see my hesitation; they had to believe I had a legitimate reason to be here.

"I've got to speak with someone in charge," I shouted, coming to a stop in front of the door.

"About what?" One of the guards asked.

"Returning something to one of your men."

"What might that be?"

"I'd like to speak to the officer in charge, so I can be sure that the right person gets his item back."

The two Americans looked at each other, then one of them nodded and disappeared inside.

A short while later he returned, another man in tow, a low-ranking officer, having obviously just eaten a sandwich, his lips and fingers still greasy.

"What do you want?" the officer asked, eyeing my rather pitiful Hitler youth pants.

"One of your guards lent me this compass," I said, showing the man Gero's present. "I'd like to return it to him."

The man extended a hand. "Give it to me, I'll take care of it."

"That's the thing," I said, "I want to hand it to him personally. His name is Williams; he was guarding the back gate until yesterday."

The officer's brows lowered. Likely, I had interrupted his meal and was burdening him with an insurmountable task. Once again, he looked me up and down, then turned wordlessly and disappeared inside.

Unsure what to do, I lingered, committed not to let Gero's compass out of my hands. I'd rather run off and let them chase me, before I parted with my most precious possession.

"Williams was reassigned to the prison wing." He squinted, his gaze on the compass still dangling from my hand. "Prison is off limits." He gave me a sly look. "Soon, this camp will only have people like you, Nazi swine. As far as I'm concerned you can rot in here for a thousand years." His spittle almost hit my shoes as he spun around and marched off.

I watched the officer disappear inside, my mind a swirling mess. Without the guard we were lost, we'd be swallowed by the camp, lost among the real monsters of the Reich. I saw myself next to Braun, my hair long and greasy, my Hitler Youth uniform in rags. He smiled at me as he pointed to his empty eye socket, "shrapnel, an honor." In the eyes of the world I'd be like him, an evil war criminal. The building and its guards began to sway. I'd rather attempt escape and have them shoot me in the back.

When the ground steadied, I remembered Emil.

"And?" he asked when I found him in the sick barracks.

"Williams has been moved, can't help us any longer."

"What are we going to do now?"

I didn't have the strength to answer.

JULY 16, 1945

When we marched to the sick barracks the next morning, a line of American trucks snaked past us. I hadn't slept much all night, my thoughts circling around our escape. We'd been so close and now the opportunity to slip away had vanished. Williams's words returned...this place was becoming an internment camp for guys like Braun and much worse.

In my mind I saw Mother pacing back and forth the morning I'd left. Her back had been turned to me, yet I knew she'd been crying. I'd kept my distance, didn't want to be near such a 'crybaby,' hadn't even hugged her. My cheeks grew hot with shame. What if she was gone? Or I could never leave this place?

"What are all the trucks doing in here?" Otto asked. He'd gotten into the habit of walking near me.

"Prisoners, I guess." I threw a glance at Emil, whose eyelids were swollen and red from lack of sleep and who hardly seemed to have energy to lift his feet. Seeing my friend so tired and discouraged, new anger flamed. "Nasty Germans," I yelled.

Otto flinched, but remained silent. I was an asshole.

Halfway through the morning shift, the American orderly waved me over. "Someone outside to see you."

At a safe distance, Williams leaned against a light pole. "I heard you had something for me."

I shrugged. "Was a ruse, so I could find out where you'd moved to."

Williams lowered his voice. "I had no idea they were reassigning me this quickly. I still want to help."

"Better make it quick, before more of us croak." I was done being nice.

Williams gripped me by the arm. "I said I'd help *you*—not the entire class."

I'm not leaving without Emil. Aloud I said, "How?"

"I've got an idea, but I need to check a couple of things first." He turned, but then looked at me again. "Be ready tonight."

Doing what? All I did was nod.

During lunch, I took Emil aside. "Williams still wants to help. He said to be ready tonight."

Emil's brows drew together. He was getting that look again that I'd come to know so well. "I've got a bad feeling about this..."

I cringed, wishing that for once, he'd keep quiet. "If we don't leave now, we'll be part of the new prison camp, those Nazis, men like Braun, will control us once again."

Emil nodded, but I could tell he was worried.

I was lying on my bunk, fighting to stay awake. Fatigue whispered to me, invited my bones to grow heavy and my eyes to close. Last night had been sleepless and the day had done nothing to calm my nerves.

Around the time we returned to our barracks for dinner, I'd discovered Williams lingering near the hospital. He nodded and turned on his heels, which I understood as an invitation to follow. Between two now abandoned barracks he stopped.

"A convoy is leaving tonight to pick up new provisions," he'd said. "They're going to Munich. I think I can get you on one of the trucks—or I'll try my best, anyway. Come to the hospital by 11:45. Don't be late."

Below me, Emil's breath came ragged. Once in a while his bunk creaked, so I knew he was staying awake as well.

A raven landed on my bed and demanded my compass. It cocked its head and looked at me with its beady eyes. "Give it to me," he squawked in a deep voice. "Give it to me." The next thing I knew, Emil tugged at my sleeve. Disoriented, I almost hit my head on the ceiling.

Then my plan returned with such fervor, I began to shake with adrenalin. Ever so quietly, I climbed from the bunk and followed Emil outside. I imagined the raven watching me. The adrenalin turned into dizziness; the bird meant death for sure. I grabbed the doorframe to steady myself, afraid to warn Emil.

Clouds raced past a half moon, though it was easy enough to see with the nightlights on the barracks. Each of us carried a tiny bundle with an extra shirt, a set of underwear and socks—I'd decided to leave my suitcase behind, didn't want it to slow me down.

We crept behind the hospital barracks and waited. Across the parade ground—a huge space where prisoners used to line up for roll call—two covered trucks stood, a handful of soldiers loading boxes into them.

"What are they doing?" Emil asked.

"No idea. Williams only said they were going to Munich." Fighting down the memory of the raven and worried about the time, I scanned the long squat building, where the former German oppressors had registered prisoners and confiscated their clothes and personal items. From our hiding spot to the trucks, we had to cross more than seven hundred feet of open ground.

"Over here." The voice seemed disembodied, but I recognized it as Williams's. He'd kept his word, but when we hurried to meet him, he froze. "I told you to come alone."

Unable to ask Williams or confide in Emil, I'd not mentioned anything. My heart hammered in my throat. "If you have a friend who's done everything with you, you wouldn't leave him behind, would you?"

Williams remained silent. In my mind, minutes ticked by. Any moment the trucks would leave—without us.

"Fine then. Get to the other side of the barracks, cross the main path, go to the end of those barracks and wait there until I wave to you—"

Cautious footsteps could be heard, then Otto's voice, "I'm coming with you."

I recoiled—*damn,* Otto's timing was perfect.

A noticeable shiver ran through Williams. "That wasn't the deal," he hissed. "If a lot of you are gone, I'll be found out. This is stupid." Abruptly, he turned and marched off.

I could've strangled Otto with my bare hands right then, but I was too close to getting away. I rushed after the guard, calling to him in a low voice, "Williams, please wait. I didn't know, I swear. Otto must've heard something, he sleeps near us. Please...he's had a hard time, worse than me...he's my friend."

My voice failed me, but I was beyond caring what was proper or if I sounded brave or strong or smart.

Maybe it was my pathetic plea or this place that was peeling away our humanity, but either way, Williams' steps slowed and then stopped.

I'd caught up to him, but in the shadow of the hospital

building I couldn't see his expression. "All right, I believe you. Get your asses down there, on the quick. Wait for my signal. If you get caught, I don't know you."

Somehow, we made it a hundred yards to the end of the hospital barracks, then across the path, to the other row of barracks, another hundred yards—Otto noisily huffing and scrambling behind us.

We had reached the end of the building—me peeking around the corner—when I noticed Williams speaking to three service men in front of the admin building. He was facing us, the backs of the soldiers to us. In the gloom from the building lights it was hard to tell if he was nodding or making some other sign.

We still had to cross the parade ground, a good seventy yards wide, to reach the trucks.

Otto was tugging at my shirt and Emil breathed in my ear. I couldn't take it any longer. Keeping my eye on Williams, I hissed something like "now" and sprinted toward the first truck. Nothing had ever seemed to take as long as running exposed across a dusty field of misery.

I heard Otto behind me, his breath way too loud in the stillness of the night. Williams' voice grew louder, he laughed and the men joined in. Then one of them said something and half turned toward us.

Panic had already made my legs so soft, my knees were pudding. Now I made a split-second decision and threw myself to the ground. Emil and Otto followed, but I knew Otto was way slower than us, his movements clumsy as if a puppeteer were pulling his limbs in different directions.

From my low vantage point I saw how Williams was waving his arms, speaking quickly. The American once again turned toward him. Now I realized what he was holding: keys...likely keys for the truck. I scrambled back to my knees and hurdled toward the small caravan. Now we were hidden behind the trucks, but when I lifted the tarp, I noticed that the entire back was stacked with boxes. There was no room, not even for a dog, not to mention three boys.

Emil and Otto had seen it too, their eyes large with fright. I pointed toward the second truck, which was dangerously close to the men talking. They'd see us. But what choice did I have?

The tarp on this one wasn't attached yet, and there were a few feet of space at the end. The rest of the platform was stacked like the other truck: to the ceiling. No way we could sit there in full view. The only way we could make it work was, if we moved some of the boxes, and climbed behind them.

One last look at Williams—he was talking, smiling and somehow nodding his head at the same time—I climbed into the truck. Emil and Otto followed, Emil helping Otto regain his balance. Thanks to the tarp, it was almost completely dark—too dark to work.

No matter. I gripped a box and moved it to the very end of the platform—then another. Touching and feeling my way around, I yanked down another, then another. Emil moved next to me to help. My lungs seemed to burst from the effort and yet, I managed to listen to the sounds outside, waiting for a sign that the men were coming.

It wasn't enough to move a few boxes; we had to create space behind them. Sweat poured beneath my shirt and my hands grew slippery. Otto tried helping, but dropped one of the boxes. Luckily, it fell only a few feet and landed on another box. Still, there was a perceptible thump. I paused, trying to listen and breathe at the same time.

In the end it didn't matter because if we didn't hurry, we'd be sent to the camp's prison or worse. There was no telling who was in it after the Americans were bringing in German war criminals.

We managed to move enough boxes to create a space for the three of us. It wasn't enough room to lie down or to even sit comfortably, but maybe we could do more, once the trucks were moving.

Outside, footsteps crunched in the gravel, voices called something in English.

Time was up. I yanked at Emil's sleeve, pulled Otto by the arm. Quickly, we climbed across the barrier of boxes now three feet tall. Ideally, we should've built a high wall again. A quick look across would expose us.

Light fell into the truck as the tarp was lifted. The three of us squeezed in the small space, Otto's wheeze loud in my ears.

The engine began to rattle as the tarp was fastened. Moments later, the truck began to move. I held on to the compass around my neck, rubbing it so furiously, my thumb ached.

Twice more the trucks slowed, then accelerated again. I let out a sigh and straightened.

"We better fix this up. No idea how long we'll be driving."

"Where're we going?" Otto asked, barely audible over the engine.

"Munich."

"How will we get away without being seen?" Anxiety made Otto's voice quiver.

I said nothing. All this time I'd worried about getting away. I hadn't even given it a second's thought, how we could climb out unseen. If we'd been in the first truck, the driver of the second would've discovered us for sure.

"Do we know where they're taking these boxes?" Emil said. "Cause if it's going to a military base, we won't be able to escape. They'll send us right back here."

Over my dead body. Aloud I said, "It'll have to be on the

road, some place where they slow down.

"I'll break my neck, jumping from a moving truck," Otto whined.

I took a deep breath, searching for patience, trying in vain to recall a map of southern Germany.

"I don't think Munich is very far from Dachau, maybe less than an hour," Emil said, confirming my suspicion.

"Then we better get ready." Without waiting for an answer, I moved to the back of the truck and tugged on the tarp. It was fastened from the outside. Damn. "Does anyone have a knife?" I said when I felt the presence of my classmates next to me.

Silence. Damn.

"I've got a nail," Otto said. "Found it yesterday."

Soft fingers pushed something at me. By the feel of it, the nail was rusty, but at least six inches long and fairly thick. Gripping it in my fist, I drove it into the canvas. And again. The material was tough, like sail cloth with some kind of wax sealant.

The other problem was that the tarp bulged outward under the force, so that I couldn't be sure, if I ever hit the same spot.

"Hold it tight," I called over the engine noise. Hopefully, the driver couldn't hear us.

Emil and Otto moved to my side and pushed against the cloth. I shoved again and again, until I had a finger-sized hole. Since my arm was about to fall off, Emil took over. He ripped and tore, making slow progress—much too slow for my taste. Already I noticed houses along the street.

The hole had grown to fist size.

"Hold on," Otto said, sticking his foot through. Then he pushed down. There were advantages to weight. The canvass tore almost to the bottom, where it was sewn double. If we were careful, we'd be able to squeeze through, but certainly not while the damn truck was moving.

And then the unthinkable happened. The truck slowed, then stopped. Voices could be heard outside and inside the truck—we'd arrived.

After a couple of exchanges, the truck moved again. Through the slit in the tarp I made out a gate with a boom, low brick buildings, a few tents and all sorts of American Army vehicles.

We were prisoners once more.

JULY 17, 1945

Standing behind that tarp, Emil, Otto and I froze. Any moment they'd discover the torn canvass. What would the Americans do with us? Send us back to Dachau? Shoot us for trying to flee? My mind was about to take off in a wild jumble, imagining all kinds of scenarios, when the truck's engine began to rattle anew.

"What's going on?" Emil asked.

I said nothing, trying to catch a glimpse through the slit in the tarp. The buildings receded as the truck stopped once more at the gate and then left.

"Quick," I cried. "Let's enlarge the hole."

Grabbing each side of the canvas, we pulled as hard as we could. The fabric gave suddenly, lengthening the tear upward. Now we had a chance. I stuck my head through the opening and scanned the streets. In the near blackness it was impossible to make out the road's surface.

"Listen," I said. "The next time the truck slows, we need to jump. Emil, you go first, then Otto, I'll be last."

"Maybe I should be last," Otto said.

I threw him a glance and even though it was mostly

dark, he got the message.

Wiggling from foot to foot, we waited. I kept one hand in the tear, so I had a view of the outside. As the truck turned, mountains of rubble appeared on each side of the road and the truck began to slow. Emil fell against me and we all gripped for something to hold on to. Judging by the rumbling and shaking, the street had to be terribly rough.

The truck stopped.

I pushed Emil toward the opening. "Out." He climbed through and disappeared from view. Then came Otto…more awkward and slow. Just as he climbed down, the truck began to move again.

No time, my brain screamed. I quickly stepped through, searching for a foothold on the outside. The truck shook and bucked, catapulting me into the night.

I flew…crash-landed on my side. Stars appeared in my vision, but all I could think of was to confirm that the trucks were leaving us behind.

"You all right?" Emil's face floated above me. "Can you move your legs, arms?"

I looked at him as the memory of our escape and my flight flooded back. My shoulder screamed and the side of my head felt kind of cottony. In the dawn light, I made out the dust-covered rubble of brick, concrete and bent steel behind which ruins rose high. I was lying with my back against the remains of a house wall.

I carefully moved my limbs, everything seemed to work.

I sat up, exploring the goose egg on my temple. "Bruised my side pretty good, still got my head."

Emil grinned. "We made it."

I grinned back. "We did." I looked past Emil, where in the early morning light a couple of women were sifting through the debris. "I didn't think we would, not after that dream."

Emil's dark eyes focused on me. "What dream?"

I shuddered. "A huge raven sat on my bunk and wanted my compass." My fingers slipped anxiously to the leather strap on my chest. "He talked like a person. I thought we were going to die for sure. He was scary...I thought..."

A huge grin spread over Emil's face. "I wish you'd told me."

"What?"

"Your raven dream." Emil chuckled. "It's a good thing. Ravens are smart and powerful. He was bringing you change, a new destiny."

I thought of Daniel and how he'd taught me to hope, and Gero, who'd convinced me that I was going home. Maybe they'd sent the raven. Managing a grin, I realized that we were alone. "Where's Otto?"

"Organizing food."

"You let him go? He's liable to get lost or arrested."

"He wanted to."

I came to my knees, painfully, then straightened. Coated in dust, I looked as if I'd jumped into a bin of flour. "How long was I out?"

"Not long, maybe—"

"Look, what I found." Otto rushed up to us, his arms loaded with three unlabeled tin cans, a jar of what looked like red jam and a half a loaf of dark bread. "There's a well not too far, where we can drink and wash."

He looked at me through his round glasses. "Glad you're up. I...we were worried." He paused. "We're definitely in Munich. North is that way." He pointed up the street.

And so began our trek home.

EPILOGUE

We arrived in Herten nearly two months after our escape from the Americans. We had walked most of the way, past broken down cars, charred remains, mountains of rubble and—the worst for me—silhouettes of bombed-out buildings. Like ragged teeth, they stuck into the sky, their windows empty eye sockets. And over everything lay dust like a death cloak.

Kind women gave us bread; often we begged and stole. The entire way I could only think of one thing: seeing my mother, wishing, hoping and praying, she was alive. While we'd sat like blind idiots in youth camp, Germany had disappeared around us. Many towns were so flattened, they were hardly recognizable. Only some of the smaller places appeared to be unscathed.

Little children, no more than five or six, were sifting through rubble, their faces so dirty one could hardly distinguish their noses. They went about their business with stoic expressions as if it were completely normal to work like slaves, instead of sitting in a sandbox building castles.

Emil, Otto and I hardly spoke. Sure, we mentioned when

183

we had to pee or couldn't stand the hunger any longer. It turned out, Otto wasn't half bad. He went to scavenge and often returned with some kind of prize: a couple of potatoes or carrots. One time he returned bare-chested, having filled his shirt with the most glorious purple grapes.

The morning we entered Herten, it drizzled. A chill lay over the town and over my heart. Like the rest of the country, the town had suffered, but not nearly as bad. Here and there houses had crumbled, but many of the neighborhoods seemed to be intact.

At some point Otto stopped, his expression pensive. "Going home," he said.

I pressed his hand. For Otto, home meant his aunt, an old spinster, who had watched over him while his mother was in the asylum. "Take care of yourself—maybe we'll see you in school?"

Otto nodded and cleared his throat. "Sure, eh, I never thanked you." His cheeks flushed as he drew an almost unrecognizable handkerchief from his pocket. "You helped me see that people can change. It gave me hope." He grinned a watery smile. "You saved my life—at least twice."

To my surprise, my throat closed up. Isn't it strange how the smallest gesture, often done without much thought can make such a difference for somebody else? There'd been a time when I'd despised Otto—didn't want to help. But he was a guy like us and just because he looked different, didn't mean he had no feelings.

"Listen, I'm sorry, I was stupid sometimes. I'm glad you came along. Stay in touch, will you?"

Otto nodded earnestly and as he turned, said, "I'm sure your mom will forgive you."

I stared after him as he picked his way across a cobblestoned street, Otto's words echoing through my head. How had he known about the fight with my mother?

I hadn't even told Emil.

"Ready?" Emil's dark eyes seemed huge in his face.

Had he had another dream and was afraid to tell me? Remembering the raven, I shook off the feeling of unease and boxed my friend in the arm. "Let's go."

I hardly remember the last minutes, entering our neighborhood...the street I'd spent my childhood on.

"Houses are all right." Emil sounded breathless.

I scanned the front of our apartment building. Indeed, it seemed fine. My feet moved faster, I began to run...sprint.

Emil was doing the same. He passed me and crossed the street to his home. The last I saw of him was his shirt disappearing in the entrance.

My heart skipped as I scanned the nametags next to the doorbell, stopped on the one with my name.... I rang, my forefinger wiggled as if possessed. *Come on, breathe.* My ears straining, I waited...for the tiniest sound, a creaking door, steps, some movement.

When the buzzer sounded, I winced and raced up the stone steps to the second floor. And there was my mother in an old dress. But that didn't matter, because I zoomed in on her face and her expression as it turned from slightly annoyed at the intrusion to sheer wonder.

"Mother," was all I could manage.

"Arthur."

I was in her arms, holding on to her so tightly, she let out a shriek. I let go a little, but only enough to stick my face against her shoulder. When had she become so short?

When we drew back, we were both crying and laughing.

"I'm sorry," I said. "I was stupid...our fight, you were right."

Mother gripped my hands and pulled me inside. Her expression was furtive, almost as if I were a ghost and she were afraid I'd evaporate any moment. "You are here, that's all that matters."

She closed the door, taking in my appearance. I think I must've looked like the lowliest street dog, my clothes so ragged and dirty, they'd lost their color. She'd grown thin, looked haggard and...old. Gray streaked her hair, and the lines around her mouth were deep as the grooves in a field. She wiped her face, shook her head.

"I'm so glad," she started. But then she ran out of words because all she did was look at me in wonderment. Her palm touched my cheeks, smoothed back my hair. "What happened to you?"

What indeed? How could I answer that question? How could I possibly explain how the war started for me when it was over for the country? I didn't, couldn't. Not then, not ever...until that fateful afternoon in the car repair shop, when I met a woman who could've been my daughter.

Why I told her what I couldn't speak of all my life, I don't know. All I can say is that I'm glad I did. For me, but more so for the others...for Daniel and Gero, Emil and Otto—my friends. And for those other classmates who didn't manage to escape with me—even Udo who refused to see the truth.

As for my soul, I can say, it returned to me when I rejoined Mother that day. Once in a while, when the clouds of my memories grew too dark, when it became too difficult to concentrate on the task of living, my soul took off for a bit. But never like it had, never long.

And as I learned to lay my past to rest—most of the time—it remained steadfastly inside me.

RETURN

July 1945

I squatted near the collapsed walls of a former villa while Helmut dug underneath a sideboard—all that remained of a kitchen. We were searching for valuables, anything suitable to trade on the black market.

When tires screeched and a truck door slammed shut, I flinched. The weeks in the woods had left their mark. I had nightmares of Birdsnest, the SS officer, chasing me through the woods and making me kneel before he put a pistol into my mouth.

I knew Helmut felt the same, his cheekbones even sharper, his fingers like sticks. We never talked about our time on the run, but the memories were always there like some evil ghost lurking over our shoulders.

"What are you boys doing?" a voice yelled in broken German.

I looked up from the rubble. "Searching for stuff."

"It's forbidden to remove items from bombsites." The man wore a British military uniform and waved a rifle.

I kept my eyes on the gun and the man's pistol on the

leather belt. "We didn't know."

"This is city property. Read the announcements." The soldier sounded irritated. As Helmut and I scrambled down the street, the officer yelled after us. "Next time I'll arrest you."

"At least he doesn't know our names," I panted as I slumped behind a fence, ignoring the rumbling in my middle. Dinner was a long time away.

"Or where we live."

"Now, what? I've got to get firewood."

"So we go back?"

I shrugged. I refused to be afraid. "Maybe another place. Surely, they can't have guards everywhere. Half the town is in ruins."

"I can't believe we are *forbidden* to take anything."

"How are we supposed to survive?"

"Exactly."

"Next they'll tell us when to use the bathroom."

"They'll have an administrator of shit," Helmut sneered.

"A *commissioner* of outhouses and water closets."

Helmut scratched his head. "I need firewood, too. We're almost out."

I grinned. "I know a place with a collapsed roof." Unlike trees, roof trusses burned long and hot.

"We'll need saws."

"Wait at the corner, I'll get them." I raced off. At least my house still stands, I mused as I approached our apartment building.

A handsaw and ax tucked under my shirt, I yelled into the kitchen, "*Mutter*, I'll be back in an hour."

The knock on the door startled me. Why didn't Helmut wait at our meeting place as usual? Irritated I yanked open the door.

"What? I thought you were—"

The visitor looked alien. Blackish filth covered his skin as if he'd spent years in a coalmine. His pants, held up by a piece of cord, were ripped, his shirt peppered with holes. Sores festered on arms and chin.

"It's me," the figure said.

With a pang I recognized the voice of my older brother, Hans.

"*Mutter*, come quick," I cried, my eyes glued to the strange figure. "Oh… come in." I motioned my skeletal brother into the house, searching for something to say. My throat was strangely hoarse. "Man, you stink. How are you?"

Hans grimaced through the muck. "Much better now that I'm home."

"Hans!" As Mother hugged my brother, I tried to hide my shock. Hans looked like a scarecrow left to rot in the field. His once muscular arms were thin as sticks, his skin loose wrinkles. He seemed to have trouble standing.

Mother wiped away a tear. "Let's get you cleaned up. Günter?"

"I'm right here."

"Fetch water, enough to fill the tub. Better go twice."

I dropped the saws and snatched our buckets instead. Anything was better than watching the crumpled figure in the kitchen. I'd catch Helmut on the way. Firewood would have to wait.

Hans had left last October, drafted as part of the early *Volkssturm*, the people's storm, Hitler's last attempts of fueling the war with Germany's adolescents. Six months later I'd been part of that same campaign. But unlike me, Hans hadn't been able to run and hide. He'd joined a tank detail as a radioman…. In February, when we'd visited him, he'd been healthy, even somewhat content. What had happened to him?

We helped Hans into the bath. In former times I would've been embarrassed to see him naked. Now I didn't care. My brother reminded me of a child, helpless and weak.

"Hand me that soap," Mother said. "And get a second brush."

I hurried into the kitchen to get a scrub brush we used for potatoes. "Where is the damn brush?" I cried, digging beneath the sink. I tossed dish clothes and towels on the floor until I found the stupid thing beneath a linen sack.

Hans had closed his eyes and lay back. I counted his ribs as I worked on his shoulders and chest. Everything was black as if he'd rolled in coal dust. Except it wasn't loose dirt, it adhered to his skin like glue.

"Are you hurt?" I asked, picking dead lice from his skin.

Hans didn't seem to hear. He just leaned into my arm like a baby.

Mother sent me back to heat more water so we could wash his head. It took an hour to see skin again. Hans never uttered a word. He only cried out a few times when we'd disturbed one of the many sores. I closed my eyes several times because I didn't want Siegfried, who'd snuck in to take a look at big brother, to see my tears.

We wrapped Hans in a towel and half carried, half dragged him into our bedroom. Hans's old clothes, mother had dug out of the dresser, hung on him in folds. I gave him my spare belt or he'd have lost his pants. After we fed him a bit of bread and peppermint tea, he crawled under the covers and passed out.

Though I was relieved Hans was safe, I soon longed to be outside and away. With ever dwindling rations, I'd hoped Hans would help *organize* supplies. With an extra mouth to feed, we urgently needed provisions because three months after the war, stores remained closed.

The Brits had taken over the management of Solingen from the Americans in late May and supposedly we were all getting plenty of rations. That is…on paper. We got coupons for everything, but Germany was in such a mess that little food reached us.

But a cloud hung wherever Hans went. At dinner he shuffled into the kitchen as if he were eighty.

"I've got to find more food," I said, poking my spoon into the watery soup with shreds of potatoes and a few onion rings.

"Maybe I should go to speak with the British administration," Mother said. But one of us has to stay with Siegfried. Her gaze fell on Hans who stared into space, seemingly having forgotten his soup.

"Hans?" I said a bit too loudly.

He jumped, then mumbled something before he met my eyes. "What?"

"You think you can stay with Siegfried while we run errands?"

"Sure," he said.

As we continued our discussion about where to unearth enough nourishment to feed four people, Hans remained silent. The next day wasn't any better. Or the next. He slept most of the time or sat forlornly in the living room. Sometimes he picked up a book, but it sat in his hands unopened.

All we knew was that he'd been captured by the British Army in early 1945 and walked home hundreds of miles from somewhere north.

"Helmut and I are going tonight," I said a week later, staring at the kitchen table scrubbed clean and polished as if it demanded food. It was my way of saying we'd steal. What choice did we have? Our pantry was empty and despite what we'd been through, I wasn't ready to starve to death.

Hans nodded. "I'll come."

I glanced at my brother, hoping the dread creeping into my stomach was unfounded. "We go after dark. It's safer. People are roaming all over the place. I'll tell Helmut."

A half-moon threw shadows across our path. The air smelled fragrant of grasses and blossoms, nature's indifference to the destruction around us. Summer had begun in earnest, lulling us with blue skies and warm temperatures. We found a handful of red currants in a front yard, the acidic fruit making me even hungrier.

When we stopped at the edge of a field of dark, leafy plants, I bent low to investigate. "You know what this is?" I whispered, barely containing my excitement.

Helmut sank to his knees. "My feet are killing me." He'd grown again during the year and was much taller than Hans and I.

"Sugar beets." I fingered the leaves. "They've been left for the second season, so they'll be sweeter. Otherwise, they wouldn't be this big yet." I yanked at a stalk. The leaves tore, the root remaining in the earth. "*Scheiße!*"

"Are we going to cook them?" He'd taken off one of his shoes, a big toe poking through the weave.

"Molasses, you idiot," I snapped, tired of being in charge. I'd kept my cool all through the hike, even though we had to stop a hundred times for Hans to catch up.

"Hmmm, molasses." My brother's voice easily carried across the field.

"Shhh," I hissed. "The farmhouse is probably close."

"Let's hurry then." Helmut began rummaging through his pack in search of a sack.

I picked up a pointed rock to dig. It had been dry for

weeks and the earth was hard and clumpy. My shirt was drenched with sweat as the pile of beets grew slowly.

I glanced at Hans, who sat motionless. "Why don't you help?"

A dog barked. I froze as memories of the old man and Rudy returned. Chances were we'd be bitten this time...or worse.

There, more sounds: twigs breaking and heavy footsteps. I bit back a curse and crept backward into a stand of hazelnut bushes, dragging the beet sack with me. Helmut followed, remembering his shoe at the last second.

"Who's there? Damn thieves!" A voice drifted through the brush to our right. "You're stealing my crop." A shot rang out.

"Where's Hans?" I peeked through the leaves. Now free of clouds, the moon bathed the field in bluish light. And right where we'd dug, my brother sat unmoving.

To my horror, a man appeared next to Hans, rifle in hand. "What're you doing in my field?" he growled. The farmer had to be in his seventies. He was bald with the ruddy skin of a life spent outdoors. "Answer me!" he said. "I should shoot you on the spot." His dog snarled as if to emphasize the point.

Hans's voice floated across the field. "Why don't you? I don't care. I've had worse."

"What are you doing in my field?" the farmer asked again.

"Taking a few beets."

I held my breath, watching...waiting. Sweat rolled down my temples and chest. I'd never forgive myself if Hans got hurt—even if he was positively crazy. Eyes on the dog, I got to my knees. I had to show myself, confess to the farmer that it'd been *my* idea.

"Son, how old are you?" the old man was just saying.

"Almost eighteen."

"You alone?" The farmer scanned the dirt which showed the fresh marks of dug-up roots.

Hans remained silent. As I shifted my weight, the dog's ears perked up and it growled. I wanted to run then, but I knew I'd never run again. Hans needed me.

"You been in the war?" The farmer's voice had lost its hostility.

"Yes."

"Thought so." With a sigh the man set down his rifle. "Listen, son. You shouldn't run around at all times of night. You'll get yourself killed. Just because the war is over doesn't mean it's safe."

Hans said nothing.

Why don't you move? Do something. I felt the same sense of paralysis as my brother, my limbs fused to the earth.

To my surprise, the farmer stiffly dropped to his knees and began to yank and twist at the leaves, the bulbous roots pulling out easily. He stuffed the beets into Hans's arms. "Take these and go home. Don't come back. Next time you may not be so lucky."

Hans awkwardly straightened and stumbled into the bushes. He kept walking, having seemingly forgotten about us as the farmer, the dog by his side, walked off in the opposite direction.

"Over here," I whispered.

"I can't believe this," Helmut said. "He got the beets for free. Didn't even have to dig."

"Let's go." I raced to catch up with my brother. "I'll help you carry."

As the gray of dawn crawled across the sky and the air begin to fill with the song of birds, we climbed up a steep hill. I kept glancing at my brother, who strained to breathe and grew slower by the minute. *He used to be strong and order me around. Now I'm the leader.* Somehow I resented Hans's slowness.

When the land flattened, Hans threw himself on the ground, his face pale as the birch bark behind him.

"You all right?" I said.

"Fine."

"You don't look fine."

Hans blinked, his eyes shiny. "Leave me alone." He rolled on his side, turning his back to me.

I tried to control my temper. It didn't work. "You could've been killed," I fumed. "Next time we'll go without you."

"You almost got *us* caught," Helmut said. "And shot."

Hans remained silent as if he hadn't heard.

I shrugged in frustration and grabbed the beets. "Let's go home. It isn't far now." Hans didn't budge. Running out of patience, I tapped him on the shoulder. "Come on."

My brother jerked and slapped hard at my hand, his eyes wild. "Ouch! Why did you punch me?"

Hans's eyes widened as he focused on me. "Sorry. I thought…"

I rubbed my fingers. Hans was a crazy man with slumped shoulders and worn eyes.

Helmut straightened. "I'm starving."

I tapped a foot in frustration. Hans still hadn't moved. It was worse than caring for my little brother.

"Wonder what happened to him?" Helmut pointed a forefinger to his temple.

Hans sighed and mumbled something.

"Why don't you tell us?" I said.

Hans shook his head. In the silence something rustled in the underbrush. Tired of waiting, I straightened. We'd have to take turns carrying my brother. We needed to get home.

But when I looked back down, Hans was muttering. "...Brits got us near the Belgian border. ...marched northeast to *Mecklenburg*." Staring into the lifting darkness, his voice turned mechanical.

"Mostly boys like me without experience—stupid. The older men got treated worse. Some were shot on the spot." He fell silent. It had been the longest he'd spoken since his return.

Helmut picked up the beets. "Let's go."

I glanced at my friend and put a finger to my lips. "Where did you sleep?" I asked turning my attention back to Hans.

"In a field with watch towers and barbed wire. We dug holes in the ground to live. We'd fight over bits of cardboard or fabric to line the bottoms. When it rained, the holes filled with mud."

I spat out a blade of grass. "That must've been terribly cold."

"Sometimes we got wood. We stripped the trees until they looked as bare as black bones."

I slumped down, eyes on my brother's back. "How large was the camp?"

"Thousands. Many died. There were mass graves." Hans slowly sat up and selected a stick from the ground, chewing gingerly. I knew his teeth were loose. "Once you got diarrhea it was over. Men just collapsed in the latrines."

"What did you eat?"

Hans grimaced. "We received a couple of biscuits most days, sometimes a handful of dry beans."

"Beans? What did you do with them?"

"We'd cook—if we had firewood." Hans leaned back with a sigh. "In the beginning when I made it up into a tree I lost the wood. I'd drop the branches on the ground and somebody would grab them and run."

"I would've punched them," I said, a fresh knot of anger forming in my stomach.

"They threw you in the box for fighting."

"What box?" Helmut interjected. He sat down, his back against a tree.

"A metal container, windowless. You couldn't stand upright or lay down for that matter. Some people were in there for weeks." Hans stared into space, once again in camp. "When they came out, they walked hunched over like old men. I made friends with a boy from Frankfurt. He and I took up house together. It was safer that way because he helped protect our stuff. I'd climb on his shoulder to reach the branches."

"How did you cook?" I thought of our own travels in the spring and the gamble Helmut and I had taken. We'd circled through the woods in terrible uncertainty, waiting for the war to be over while hiding from the SS. Forty-seven days of hunger, forty-seven days of living in fear of being found out and shot.

"A tin can. You'd burn your fingers and we never got the beans very soft, but it was something warm." Hans shivered as if he were back north.

"You're safe now. We'll take care of you." A feeling of warmth spread through me as I realized I meant every word.

"What happened to your friend?" Helmut asked.

Hans turned paler, his chin quivering.

"We better take you home." I held out my hand at a safe distance. Hans ignored it.

"My friend is dead," Hans mumbled. "He was trying to help me and they pushed him down."

"The Brits?"

"Some gang. Rough fellows. They took whatever they wanted. Real criminals. One of them stole my cup. It was enamel and better for cooking. I'd traded a load of wood for it. My friend came to help get it back, but they threw him on the ground. He hit his head on a rock. He lay there, bleeding and nobody did a thing." Hans's eyes glittered.

"Couldn't you run away?" Helmut said.

"Some tried. They were shot." Hans wiped a sleeve across his face.

"Damn war." I watched my older brother whose face looked pinched as if his skull had shrunken along with his muscles. "Let's go home and eat."

Hans ignored me and began to tremble. "Why?" he blurted.

"Why what?" My stomach beyond growling, I wanted to yank Hans to his feet.

"Hitler meant to kill us all." Despite its low tone, Hans's voice seethed. "They knew and didn't care. My friends are dead. My classmates...dead. For what?"

I chewed my lip. What could you say when your own country had betrayed you, sending its fifteen- and sixteen-year olds to be slaughtered, the most evil government of mankind. Looking down at my brother, I felt his sadness and fury like my own. Wordlessly, I held out a hand.

Hans finally took it.

As I sat down for breakfast, the first rays of sun reached their bright fingers through the window. My hands showed traces of mud, my pants were stained, and I yearned for a bath.

"We'll have to keep an eye on him," Mother said after I told her about Hans. "I wish your father were home."

I nodded, not trusting myself to speak. Pressure built in my throat every time I thought of my father. I swallowed, but the lump remained. The war had ended two months ago, and my father had not come home.

What if he'll act like Hans? the voice in my head whispered. *Or not return at all.*

"I can't believe the farmer *gave* Hans beets," I finally said, clearing my throat.

The sugar beet syrup looked like black gold, a heavenly combination of earth and sun melded into liquid sweetness. I licked my lips to savor each drop. I looked around the kitchen, cherishing this moment, cherishing the knowledge that Hans was safe. I would make sure it remained that way, regardless that I was the younger brother.

Across the table, Hans dribbled syrup on a piece of cornbread. His eyes were closed, his face relaxed as if he were asleep.

I smiled.

Author's Note: Sugar beet molasses are a regional specialty in Germany's Rhineland. Günter's father returned from the war, having walked on foot from the Balkans.

MAIN CHARACTERS

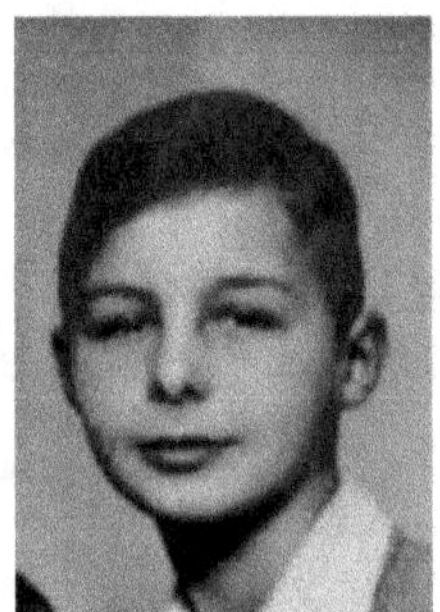

Günter 1928-

Günter became a master dye maker and ran his own company for seven years. In 1970, he joined Hugo Pott, a world-renowned silverware company and became a lead designer. His unique expertise, a combination of artistry and technical knowledge, made him a sought-after employee all his life. He had two children with his wife, Helga, and retired at age 70. Always figuring he'd be the first to die, he was devastated when Helga fell ill. After her death, he struggled to find meaning in his life, but the grit that accompanied him all his life saved him. He remains independent, still lives in the same house and is active with his nature ponds and garden.

Helmut 1928-1992

Helmut became a typesetter and had two children with his wife Helga. A heavy smoker all his life, he contracted lung cancer and passed away in 1992. Günter and Helmut remained casual friends all their lives.

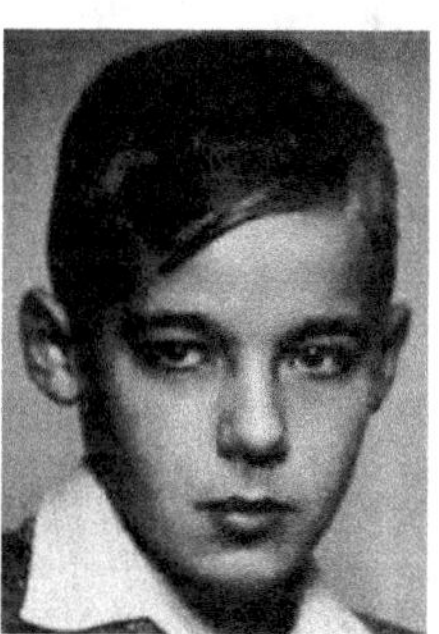

Hans 1927-2001

Hans became a commercial electrician and traveled often on business. He married another Helga – a popular name in the twenties and thirties – and had one daughter. After his wife passed away from a heart condition, he retired near Günter's home and married a second time. An avid cook and wine connoisseur, he passed away from liver disease.

Günter, Hans and Helmut after the war

TIMELINE: THE LAST MONTHS

September 11, 1944
Allied troops reach Trier, the first German town in the west.

September 17, 1944
35,000 Allies land behind the western front in Belgium, despite their numbers they fail to occupy the Rhine bridges

September 25, 1944
Hitler orders to create a Volkssturm, the people's storm, consisting of all able-bodied men between 16 and 60 years of age, to defend the country.

October 18, 1944
Official announcement of the Volkssturm. The first participants are organized and used for propaganda purposes.

November 10, 1944
Thirteen members of the youth organization 'Edelweiss

Pirates' are executed in Cologne.

November 17, 1944
To free up boys for the front, women must work the FLAK (anti-aircraft war helpers)—the FLAK was customarily done by teen boys.

December 12, 1945
Germany initiates the last defensive push in the French Ardennes—lack of supplies cause it to fail after a few days. Hitler insists to continue.

January 6, 1945
German civilians are urged to make the 'Volksopfer', the 'People's Sacrifice' to help equip the Volkssturm, which means they are supposed to donate their last possessions.

January 27, 1945
The Red Army liberates the concentration/death camp Auschwitz with 7,600 prisoners.

January 30, 1945
The Red Army sinks the passenger steamship 'Wilhelm Gustloff' in the Baltic Sea, 9,000 refugees perish.

In a radio address Hitler calls for the 'Endsieg,' the final victory and refers to the implementation of wonder weapons.

February 15, 1945
To maintain the 'fighting spirit,' the Reich's justice minister announces via radio the introduction of drumhead trials. SS, party and military members now have the right to kill military personnel *and* civilians, if they don't show enough

resolve to fight or otherwise engage in inacceptable behavior.

February 26, 1945
Additional drumhead trials are introduced as the Wehrmacht experiences record desertion.

March 5, 1945
In the desperate last wave of the Volkssturm, Wilhelm Keitel, general and head of the German Wehrmacht, adds all boys, born in 1929, to join the Volkssturm.

March 7, 1945
American troops occupy Cologne.

March 22, 1945
American troops cross the Rhine near Oppenheim and move toward Frankfurt.

March 31, 1945
Dwight D. Eisenhower stops Allied troops from advancing to Berlin, intending to leave the capital to the Red Army.

April 3, 1945
Himmler orders the immediate execution of all male occupants in houses showing white capitulation flags.

April 11, 1945
American troops liberate the concentration camp Buchenwald.

April 15, 1945
The SS forces 50,000 prisoners from two concentration

camps to participate in death marches.

April 16/17, 1945
American troops arrive in Solingen. Its citizens surrender without a fight.

April 17, 1945
German soldiers surrender in the Ruhr region, 320,000 men surrender.

April 21, 1945
Battle of Berlin, 2.5 million Red Army soldiers surround the city, fighting one million German soldiers. The last fanatics, SS, Hitler youth create stand-up desertion tribunals, shooting surrendering German citizens on the spot.

April 23, 1945
Hitler fires Reichsmarschall Goering because Goering planned to initiate negotiations with Western Allies.

April 29, 1945
American troops liberate the concentration camp Dachau.

April 30, 1945
Hitler commits suicide.

May 1, 1945
Propaganda minister Joseph Goebbels and his wife authorize a doctor to murder their six children and then commit suicide.

May 2, 1945
German troops in Berlin surrender to the Red Army.

May 3, 1945
Two German steam ships with evacuated concentration camp survivors are bombed by the British RAF. 7,000 people die.

May 2-8, 1945
The German government surrenders.

June 5, 1945
In a joint declaration the four victorious countries, France, England, the Sowjetunion and the U.S.A, declare absolute governmental power and divide Germany in four occupied zones, Berlin is divided into four sectors.

AUTHOR NOTE

The *Volkssturm* or people's storm was Hitler's last propaganda command, not organized by the German military but the NSDAP, the Nazi party. All able-bodied men between 16 and 60 were classified into four groups from most usable to least usable. My father, Günter, born in December 1928, had just turned 16 and was in classification III. Military training was supposed to take place within the Hitler Youth (HJ) by the end of March 1945. At this point in the war, allied troops had been on German ground for months, German soldiers on the retreat. Weapons and equipment were almost impossible to find. It is reported that more than 1.3 million guns were needed, but only 18,000 available. Machine guns were even more rare: 75,000 were needed and 180 available. Originally, the *Volkssturm* was supposed to defend the home front. In the case of my father, the boys were ordered to find their way about 200 km south to Marburg. I assume this was done in an attempt to stop the advancing U.S. Armies who were already in *Siegen*, less than sixty miles from Marburg. One can only imagine what happened when these youngsters were confronted with fully equipped and trained U.S. troops. Did they even have guns or did they attempt to stop tanks with their bare hands?

70% of these boys who'd grown up during the Nazi reign, volunteered. How many boys and men served during the *Volkssturm* is unknown. Their effect was negligible. They could not even protect single homes, not to mention a professional army.

To some readers it may appear that this act of defiance, of not answering conscription is nothing special. My father didn't shoot SS-men nor did he plan an assassination on Hitler. He was neither a killer nor was he in the resistance. But he did one important thing many much older and mature people neglect to do. He thought for himself. Then he took a gamble and followed through on his conviction. The way I see it, this was extremely difficult, considering how much pressure was put on the people to follow orders. In a dictatorship refusing to follow orders means certain punishment. In my father's case, it would've meant certain death because even in the spring of 1945, cells of fanatical SS-men remained and many innocent people were shot.

None of Günter's classmates were ever heard of or seen again.

While researching my WWII novels 'Surviving the Fatherland' and 'When They Made Us Leave,' I came across many stories about Germany's civilians, but I had never heard about or read anything like this one.

Arthur's tale is upsetting, sad and at times shocking. Yet, it must be told because it exemplifies additional nuances of victimization. On the one hand, Jews, minorities and people with disabilities were the first to fall prey to the Nazi regime. Communists and members of other political parties became enemies of the state.

And then there was civilian Germany. I've already written extensively about the plight of Germany's war children and youths who got caught up in the propaganda of this time and experienced a horrific war, they had no say in.

"Serves them right." How often do we say things like that, when we feel justice is being served? Some people may contend that those boys had it coming. Arguably, they may have been enthusiastic about the war at first, about fighting enemies, about believing in a great Germany. They were, after all, the product of a decade of National Socialist propaganda. And Hitler and Propaganda Minister Goebbels were excellent at influencing the nation's youth.

Yet, Arthur's story and that of his classmates takes suffering to a new level. Imagine being fifteen years old, a teenager. Imagine the horror of finding out that all you held true was a lie, and then to be faced with the atrocities of a concentration camp, and finally being forced to help alleviate the terrible evil those poor inmates had experienced? When I think about this situation—burying thousands of emaciated bodies and taking care of the sick— I wonder if those boys wished for a quick death instead.

The fact that the man I named Arthur never uttered a word about his ordeal in seventy-five years tells you, how traumatic the experience must have been.

As an author, I am used to digging up painful histories, but I admit that writing about Dachau put me to my limit. There were many a days, I had tears in my eyes. Often, I had to put down this story and create a bit of space, so it wouldn't swallow me.

I also chose to infuse a bit of kindness and hope into this story, though I do not know if Arthur experienced any. Except for the guard who helped him escape, I don't have confirmation. But having written plenty of historical and biographical novels, I know that readers crave a bit of positivity off and on.

We all can agree that the inmates of concentration camps suffered beyond comprehension, yet I marvel at the incredible strength they showed in the face of such atrocities. Humans have the unique ability to find the smallest glimpse of goodness and hold on to it, though personally, I don't know if I would've had the will to continue living.

"Germany must either be a world power or there will be no Germany," Hitler said in *Mein Kampf*. He was willing not only to sacrifice his enemies, but his own country. Because true dictators do not care about the people they are supposed to govern. My own teen parents experienced so much during and after the war, and luckily found enough strength to continue—so did Arthur and his friends.

What exactly makes one person persist a great sorrow and another succumb to its pressure and die? I do not know. I cannot explain. Some people suffer a light injury and give up; others reach the brink of death and crawl through a dessert, climb down a mountain or survive a concentration camp.

Concentration Camp Dachau

For multiple reasons, the Dachau concentration camp (KZ) has entered our collective history in infamy. On March 22, 1933, Dachau was the first KZ and prototype, a model camp, initially interning political prisoners like social democrats and communists. These prisoners were forced to work so hard that they often succumbed to exhaustion. Then followed minorities.

More than 40,000 people died in Dachau, including Jews, Sinti, Roma, German communists and social democrats, Polish and Russian prisoners of war. Even in the last days of the war, as American troops bore down on the country, the SS forced 7,000 prisoners to participate in death marches south of Munich. Over its twelve-year existence, more than 200,000 prisoners were held in Dachau.

On April 29, 1945, the U.S Army, Seventh Division, came upon Dachau and liberated the camp. Multiple reports were written, photos were taken, many of them available for review and research.

There is nothing good about Dachau—just the name sends chills down most people's backs. The only useful thing is that today Dachau is a memorial site that serves as a stark reminder of what dictatorships and its willing followers are capable of.

I fervently hope that humanity will not forget and repeat the same mistakes Germany made.

A Final Note

On the surface, the stories of Günter, Helmut, Hans, and Arthur have happy endings. All boys made it home and reunited with their mothers. But deep down, these stories also show that true happy endings are unlikely if not impossible. Some traumas are kept for life and never resolved; a person is forced to just deal with it. One of the ways Arthur dealt with it was not to talk about it ever again. My father Günter did the opposite, he talked about his experiences all the time. Helmut and Hans died rather young. The science of transgenerational epigenetic has proven one thing: we all carry the traumas of previous generations inside us.

ABOUT THE AUTHOR

Annette Oppenlander is an award-winning writer, literary coach and educator. As a bestselling historical novelist, Oppenlander is known for her authentic characters and stories based on true events, coming alive in well-researched settings. Having lived in Germany the first half of her life and the second half in various parts in the U.S., Oppenlander inspires readers by illuminating story questions as relevant today as they were in the past.

Oppenlander's bestselling true WWII story, Surviving the Fatherland, received eight nominations/awards. Uniquely, Oppenlander weaves actual historical figures and events into her plots, giving readers a flavor of true history while enjoying a good story.

Oppenlander shares her knowledge through writing workshops at colleges, libraries, festivals and schools. She also offers vivid presentations and author visits. The mother of fraternal twins and a son, she now lives with her husband and mutt Zelda in Germany.

From the Author

Thank you for reading 'Boys No More.' My sincere hope is that you derived as much entertainment from reading this story as I enjoyed in creating it. If you have a few moments, please feel free to add your review of the book at your favorite online site for feedback (Amazon, Apple iTunes Store, Goodreads, etc.). Also, if you would like to connect with previous or upcoming books, please visit my website for information and to sign up for e-news: annetteoppenlander.com.

Sincerely, Annette

Contact Me

Website: annetteoppenlander.com
Facebook: facebook.com/annetteoppenlanderauthor
Email: hello@annetteoppenlander.com
Twitter: @aoppenlander
Pinterest: @annoppenlander
Instagram: @annette.oppenlander
Blog: annetteoppenlander.com/blog/

If you are interested in getting to know Günter better, you may be interested in reading my biographical novel, Surviving the Fatherland. The story follows Günter and Helmut as well as Lilly over a period of 13 years as they grow from children to youths to adults. Eventually Günter and Lilly meet and fall in love, but the burdens they carry cast a shadow on their future—based on a true story.

Winner/Nominee of Eight Awards

PREVIEW
Surviving the Fatherland: A True Coming-of-age Love Story Set in WWII Germany

Chapter One

Lilly: May 1940

For me the war began, not with Hitler's invasion of Poland, but with my father's lie. I was seven at the time, a skinny thing with pigtails and bony knees, dressed in my mother's lumpy hand-knitted sweaters, a girl who loved her father more than anything.

It was May of 1940, my favorite time of year when the air is filled with the smell of cut grass and lilacs, promising excursions to town and the cafes in the hilly land I called home.

Like any other weekend, my father came home that Friday carrying a heavy briefcase of folders. Only this time, he flung his case in the corner of the hallway like it was a bag of garbage. You have to understand. My father is a neat freak, a man who keeps himself and everything he touches in absolute order. And so even at seven—even before he said those fateful words—I knew something was different.

My father had been named after the German emperor, Wilhelm, and Mutti called him Willi, but to me he was always Vati.

Ignoring me, he hurried into the kitchen, his eyes bright with excitement. "I've been drafted."

At the sink, Mutti abruptly dropped her sponge and stared at him. Her mouth opened, then closed without a sound.

I didn't understand what he was talking about. I didn't understand the meaning of a lie, yet I felt it even then. Like others detect an oncoming thunderstorm, pressure builds behind my forehead, a heaviness in my bones. There is something in the way the liar moves, his limbs hang stiffly on the body as if his soul cringes. His look at me is fleeting and there is something artificial in his voice.

At that moment I knew Vati was hiding something from us.

"They want me there Monday. I'll be a captain." His voice trembled as he sank into a chair, still wearing his coat and hat.

"But that's in three days." Mutti picked up Burkhart, my little brother who was just a toddler and had begun to whine. "It's fine," she soothed as she paced the length of the kitchen, the click-click of her heels like an accusation.

I frowned and moved closer to my father. Since my brother's birth, Mutti had been spending every minute with the baby. No matter how well I behaved, how I did what she asked, I rarely succeeded drawing her eyes away from my brother. It annoyed me to no end that I couldn't stop myself from trying.

"Vati, where are you going?" I asked, secure in the knowledge that my little brother wouldn't draw away his attention.

My father's cheeks glowed with excitement. As if he hadn't heard me, he rushed back into the hallway and knelt in front of the wardrobe. I followed.

One door gaped open, revealing a gray military uniform. He was rummaging below.

"What are you looking for?"

"Just a minute." He emerged with a pair of shiny black boots.

He knelt at my level and to this day I remember smelling the cologne he used every morning, a mix of spice and citrus.

"I am packing."

"Where are you going?" Vati had never been away, not even for one night. In fact, he and Mutti had strict routines, and these were dictated by the clock. We ate every night at six thirty sharp. Even on Sundays. Breakfast was at seven in the morning. Clothes never ever lay on the floor, each item brushed and aired and returned to its spot in the closet. Life was laid out in rules, washing hands before dinner, carrying a clean handkerchief at all times and always, always looking spotless when leaving the house.

He smoothed the pants of his uniform. "I'll be helping out in the war."

"Will you be back for my birthday?" My birthday was on

June fourth and I worried about our customary visits to town. In the window of *Wiesner*, our local toy store, I'd discovered a *Schildkröt* doll. Her name was Inge and I wanted her badly. Vati said she looked just like me, with blond hair and this pretty red-checkered dress with a white apron and white patent shoes you could take off.

As Vati lifted me in the air and turned in a circle, I shrieked in surprise and delight. I was flying.

"They want me after all! With all my experience, they should be glad."

Mutti put Burkhart on the floor and leaned in the doorframe to the kitchen, her arms folded across her chest. "I wish you didn't have to go."

"It's not so bad, Luise." Vati gripped her shoulders as if he wanted to infuse his excitement into her. "I'll be back soon. We're so much stronger than last time."

"All I see is Hitler sending more men into battle. Do you at least know where you're going?"

Vati shrugged. "Probably France or Scandinavia."

"Will you be back soon?" I tried again.

He patted my head and returned to his chair at the head of the table. "I'll be home before you've found time to miss me." As he began to whistle, something nagged my insides like a tiny clawing animal.

A screeching wail erupted. Sharp and metallic, it cut through doors and walls and echoed through the streets. No matter that the siren blasted every day, it made me shiver.

I watched my mother freeze, her eyes filled with something I would soon learn to recognize as fear. The siren continued—up, down, up, down. Another wail erupted. This time it sounded like the foghorn of a ship, signaling the end of the alarm.

Relieved that the horrible noise was over, I climbed on

my father's lap, running a forefinger across the bluish stubble of his jaw. "Vati?"

"Not now, Lieselotte, we are talking," Mutti said.

I looked up in alarm. Mutti had said Lieselotte when everyone called me Lilly, a sure sign she was mad. I slid back off, keeping my hand on Vati's arm.

Mutti tucked a strand of pale hair behind her ear and slumped into a chair. "I hate these air raid sirens."

Vati didn't look up from the newspaper. "It's just a test… a precaution."

Mutti abruptly straightened. "I should work on dinner. You *do* remember that my brother is visiting tonight?" Two red spots that didn't quite match her lipstick glowed on her cheeks. "Lilly, there's honey all over this table. Wash out the dishrag and wipe this down."

"Yes, Mutti." I clumsily scrubbed the surface, glancing back and forth between my parents. Vati's eyes, usually a watery blue, sparkled like an early morning sky.

"Don't you see that this is important?" he said, letting the paper sink once more. "We're fighting against England and France, even Scandinavia! Our country needs us."

"You mean they need you."

"Everyone has a role to play."

"They didn't ask me if *I* wanted to play a role." Mutti's voice was shrill as she set a pot on the stove and began to peel potatoes. "I'll be stuck with two children to take care of."

"That's exactly what the Führer wants you to do. Girls are meant to be mothers and take care of our families. We take care of the rest."

"Like your war?"

Hearing my parents argue made my insides turn knotty. I wanted them to stop, yet I finished cleaning and said nothing. All I did was return to Vati's chair as their arguments continued flying like knives above my head.

"We have to make sacrifices," Vati said. "You're a strong woman. Besides, isn't the government taking care of things? Every family receives rations, even for clothes. They're thinking of everything."

"These ration cards are so cumbersome. And the sirens drive me crazy."

Vati got up and patted Mutti's back. "Don't worry, everything will work out fine.

During dinner, I continued watching my parents. Heavy silence lingered except for my brother's babble and the scraping of spoons across porcelain bowls.

I didn't taste much of the soup. My eyes were drawn to the stony faces on either side as I recalled the events of the afternoon, wondering if I had done something to make them angry. In that stillness of the kitchen, I sensed that my life was about to change. Something dreadful lingered like a wolf lying in wait behind a bush ready to pounce. You didn't see it or hear it, yet you knew it was there.

"Tim says that women who wear lipstick are whores," I said, my gaze lingering on my mother's mouth where the remnants of lipstick clung to her lower lip.

"Who is Tim?" Mutti snapped.

"A boy in my class. His older brother is in the Hitler youth and they say girls should not paint their faces and listen to the men—"

"Young girls like yourself are pretty just the way they are," Vati said.

I was sure Tim had talked about all women and though I burned to know what a whore was, I decided to keep my mouth shut. My teacher's probing eyes appeared in my vision, and I remembered my earlier mission.

"Vati, will you read with me tonight?" I was a terrible reader, hated it, especially when I had to read aloud in class and Herr Poll slammed his ruler on my desk when I got stuck.

Mutti's mouth pressed together in a straight line as she headed for the window to pull down the blackout shutters. "Not tonight," she said. "Clear the table while I cover the other windows and change your brother. Then you get ready for bed."

Vati jumped up and disappeared in the living room. "We'll do it another time," he said before he closed the door.

As I watched Mutti carry Burkhart to bed, I felt as transparent as the air around me. But not in a comfortable way—more like a sore throat that sticks around and reminds you off and on that you're still sick.

After stacking our dishes in the sink, I followed my father, who was studying a file of papers.

"Vati?"

"What is it, Lilly?"

I hesitated. Was this a good time to ask about *Inge*, the doll? Vati was acting so strange. Even now his face had a damp shine to it as if he'd run to catch the streetcar.

"Nothing," I said. "*Gute Nacht*, Vati."

"Sweet dreams."

Disappointed, I quietly closed the door, stopping halfway to my bedroom. No sounds came from the kitchen.

I was about to climb into bed when the doorbell rang. I froze. Something bad was going to happen. Was the war coming to get Vati?

But when I heard voices in the corridor I recognized Mutti's brother, August, my favorite uncle. He always brought me gifts, a chocolate éclair, a flower from his garden or a bowl of sweet cherries.

I breathed again, growing aware of my icy feet on the

linoleum.

By the sounds they'd gone into the living room, a perfect opportunity to see my uncle and find out more about Vati's plans. If I pretended my stomach ached, maybe, just maybe I could visit for a while. I bent over my brother who was lying on his back, his mouth relaxed in sleep, blonde curls framing his face. In that moment I envied him. It wouldn't be the last time.

On the other side of the wall, Vati shouted. Alarmed, I tiptoed into the hallway and peeked through the living room door. Uncle August, his legs stretched long in front of him, lounged on the sofa next to a young woman I didn't recognize, while Mutti sat on an armchair by the window.

"I don't believe this. How can you be so enthusiastic?" August's voice rose as he spoke, at the same time patting the young woman's knee. "Don't you remember the last war? You of all people."

"Nonsense," Vati said from somewhere beyond the door. "This war will be over quickly. Our weapons are superior. I mean, Poland practically fell in a day and France and Scandinavia aren't far behind."

August shook his head, his eyes squinting. "I don't understand how you turn your back on your family." His voice was filled with disgust. "Aren't you worried about leaving your wife and children? This damn thing gives me the creeps. The SS and Gestapo are watching our every step. Just the other day—"

"Shhh," the woman next to him said. "August, please be careful. What if somebody listens?"

"I'm not turning my back," Vati shouted. "We've got to do our duty. Besides, the Führer is taking care of everyone."

August threw a glance at Mutti. "Since when can we trust the government?"

Mutti leaned forward. "The apartment below is vacant.

When Willi leaves, I won't even have a neighbor to talk to," she choked, her eyes glistening. "You want me to ask Herr Baum? He's older than Methuselah and can barely walk, let alone help if things get worse."

I cringed. I liked the old man next door, especially his knobby hands that were brown and gnarled like miniature tree trunks. He always listened when I spoke as if what I said were important.

"I'm convinced this war will be over before the year is up." Vati sounded irritated, and there was that darkness again, that fakeness in his voice. "I, for my part, am proud to help out."

August jumped up so suddenly, I nearly banged my head against the doorframe. "Well, I'm not." His eyes narrowed. "I thought your job at the city was highly important. Strange they let their top civil engineer walk off like that."

The silence that followed reminded me of dinner when my parents hadn't spoken, yet I could hear their anger as clearly as if they'd screamed at each other. I no longer wanted to go inside, yet I couldn't leave, my legs as rigid as Herr Poll's ruler.

"Either way," August continued, "all I wanted was to introduce my fiancée, Annelise. I'm sorry I came."

Mutti stood up, wiping her eyes. "Please August, don't go yet. I'm sure it'll all work out."

"That's right," Vati said, sounding calm again. "Let's drink to your engagement. I'll get a bottle of wine from the cellar."

I rushed to my bedroom and curled up tightly the way I did during thunderstorms. It took me another hour to get to sleep, my mind firmly on the image of Vati handing me the doll, Inge, for my birthday.

Chapter Two

Günter: May 1940

"Attention! Feet together, arms down, hands at your pant seams. Look straight. Stand still," the boy shouted. He was no more than sixteen, and the khaki uniform hung in folds around his narrow chest. The hair around his ears, shaved to the skin, left a tuft of blonde on top like a bird's nest.

He paced up and down in front of us, a row of eleven year-old boys, his eyes narrowed into angry slits. "Men," he yelled, "you are the future soldiers of Germany. You don't fight to die, but to win." He yanked open a book. "I quote. Nothing is more important than your courage. Only the strong person, carried by belief and the fighting desire of your own blood, will be master during danger." The book snapped shut. "I expect absolute obedience."

I stood next to my best friend, Helmut, at the sports stadium where the local Hitler youth met for drill. We'd lined up in rows of three deep in the middle of the grass-covered field. Another boy with red and blue patches on his shirt appeared in front of us.

"Tuck in your shirt, pull up your socks," he said, pointing at Helmut. "Look at the filth on your shoes. This is no way to dress. Show some pride."

From the corner of my eye, I watched Helmut adjust his shirt and rub his shoes. Helmut sometimes forgets about these things. Thankfully my own socks stretched to just below my knees. Still, I held my breath as the boy passed by. Earlier today we'd bought a uniform: black shorts and beige shirt, neckerchief with leather knot, armband, and the best part, a brand-new knife. Mother had grumbled about spending so much money.

"But Mutter, all boys have to go," I'd argued after we left the store. "They told us at school. It's our duty." I didn't tell her how excited I'd been about my new outfit. Most of the time I get the hand-me-downs from my older brother, Hans.

"What're they going to do with you?" she'd said, her voice stern with irritation.

"Make fires and camp." I didn't tell Mother that I couldn't wait trying out my new knife and going on adventures with a bunch of boys.

Now I waited in a line and couldn't move a muscle. Stupid.

"Attention! Turn left, march! One, two, one, two, follow me." Birdsnest headed down the field while the other youth observed, waiting for us to trip and fall out of line. We marched back and forth, left and right, crisscrossing the field. What a bore.

The air smelled of early summer and warmth. Dandelions and forget-me-nots dotted the grass like a colorful carpet. Imitating my classmates, I fought the urge to look around, keeping my head straight toward the horizon as if I could see what was coming a mile away.

A man in a brown uniform with a red armband watched from the sidelines. Distracted for a moment, I stepped on the heels of the fellow in front.

"Ouch," the boy yelled. "Watch yourself, idiot."

"You're the idiot. Why did you stop?" I said.

Birdsnest materialized in front of us. "What's going on here?"

"He stepped on me," the other boy said.

My cheeks felt hot. "He suddenly stopped."

"Name."

"What?"

"Your *name*."

"Günter Schmidt."

"Listen to me, Günter." Birdsnest's eyes narrowed. "Quit playing around. You're training to become a soldier. On the ground. Give me twenty pushups, quick."

"Yes, sir." I hurriedly dropped to the grass and hid my face because my head had turned into a super-heated balloon ready to fly away.

Out of breath I returned to the row, swallowing the choice words choking me. The marching continued, followed by singing:

"Our flag flies in front of us;
To the future we trek man for man,
We march for Hitler through night and adversity
With the youth's flag for freedom and bread.
Our flag flies in front of us,
Our flag is the new era,
Our flag leads us into eternity,
Yes, the flag is more than death.

Birdsnest continued reading from his book about becoming heroes, but my thoughts, sped up by the gnawing in my stomach, wandered to the dinner waiting at home. On dismissal, Birdsnest gave me a nasty look before reminding us to practice marching and standing to attention. He never mentioned camping or making fires.

Boring. We weren't allowed to use our knives either. Worse, we'd have to go again Saturday.

By the time I arrived at my house, it was late and I was in a rotten mood. Helmut is much more of a talker, but he was grumpy, too, and we'd walked home in silence.

I lived on the first floor of an apartment house on *Weinsbergtalstrasse*, one of a row of identical three-story homes. Recently built of brick and stucco, they were considered modern, each house painted the same pale green except for an occasional flower box in a white-framed window. I loved our new water closet. You pulled on the chain, which I was strictly forbidden to play with, and the water released from a tank under the ceiling, flushing everything away. Helmut still had an outhouse.

Entering our flat, I tossed my cap in the corner and headed to the kitchen. "I'm hom—"

The words stuck in my throat because the table, set for five, was untouched, the room deserted. A sense of unease crept up inside me, quickly forgotten because of the delicious smell emanating from the cast-iron pot. I lifted the lid and let out a sigh: bean soup with ham and smoked sausage. I glanced at the clock, seven-thirty. No wonder I was starving.

We never ate later than six. Something was wrong.

Reluctantly, I turned away from the soup and tiptoed down the hallway. Voices came from my parents' bedroom.

Stopping at the threshold, I knocked. "*Vater?*"

"Come in."

I cracked open the door. "Are we going to eat?"

Mother sat hunched over on the bed, my father kneeling in front of her. I wanted to enter, but something in their expressions held me back.

My father straightened with effort. "I'm leaving tomorrow."

"What do you mean?" I looked back and forth between my parents.

"I've been drafted."

I stared at him as his words echoed through my head. "But you said they needed you in the factory. You said you had more work than you could handle, making those fancy swords for the officers."

"That's what I thought." My father's voice remained steady but his jaws were tight.

"Can't you tell them you're too busy?"

My father sighed and put an arm on my shoulder, his expression serious. Despite being short, he could carry a hundred kilo sack of grain as if it were a small child. He wasn't the hugging type, but tonight he held on to me.

"That's not how it works."

"Where will you go?"

"Don't know. Maybe to Scandinavia."

Wiping her eyes, Mother stood up. "Why don't you get your brothers and eat? We'll pack and be in soon. And take off those clothes."

During the night, despite being tired, I tossed and turned. I'd burned my tongue on the soup at dinner, and my stomach was making weird noises. By the sound of it, my older brother, Hans, wasn't sleeping either.

While the radio proclaimed victories daily, news of fallen soldiers had begun to arrive, and announcements appeared in the newspaper. A square black cross was printed above each obituary and Mother grumbled and shook her head, reading the names and ages of the dead. I envisioned my father stumbling blindly toward a sea of barbwire, his head and eyes wrapped in bandages, his arms stretched in front.

Time stood still in the early morning hours as I

wondered if my father would return with limbs missing or not at all. I imagined the obituary in the paper: Artur Schmidt, died in battle. I considered asking Hans what he thought would happen, but before I could, a soft snore came from the other bed.

I turned on my back and stared into the darkness. The apartment was silent, but not the silence of peaceful sleep, rather an artificial stillness of cries muffled by pillows and of thoughts that whirled without end. I turned again, facing the wall, my last thought of my father waving to me with a rifle.

In the morning I awoke with a start. My brother's bed was a pile of sheets and blankets. Remembering last night, I sighed. Soft murmurs drifted in from the kitchen—my father's voice. I wanted to stay in bed and listen, and at the same time I wanted to be near him.

With a sigh, I jumped out of bed.

"Günter, you sleepy head." My father opened his arms. "Give me a hug."

I buried my face in the folds of my father's shirt. "Are you leaving now?" My father smelled of shaving soap, reminding me of his ritual, the razor, a single sharp blade, swiped back and forth across a leather strap to sharpen it further, the soft foamy soap and the thick brush made of badger hair, my father disappearing under a layer of white bubbles before taking the knife to scrape away the stubble.

"It's time."

Everybody crowded in. I sobbed, my throat tight and achy.

My father grabbed me and Hans by the arm. "You two need to take care of your mother and Siegfried."

I swallowed hard, the lump in my throat threatening to expand to my eyes. I knew that Hans was upset by the way his shoulders trembled. My baby brother, Siegfried, was only three and had no idea what was going on.

"I don't want to hear of any mischief. Do what you're told."

"Yes, *Vater*," I said. "When will you come back?"

"As soon as they let me."

"Promise?"

"I'll write." My father moved toward Mother. "I'll see you soon, Grete," he whispered.

Wiping his eyes with the back of his hand, he turned. For a moment he looked around the living room, the leather sofa, his favorite chair in the corner, the walnut table and matching sideboard.

A bright morning sun beamed into the room, throwing patterns on the wood. A starling trilled high of summer and new beginnings. With a final nod, my father hurried to the door—and was gone.

Mother dabbed her eyes where fresh tears kept arriving. "You heard what your father said. We better talk about your new responsibilities."

"Can't we do it after school?" My legs were heavy from lack of sleep.

Mother resolutely picked up pen and paper. "Who wants to help with laundry?"

"That's girl's work," Hans said. "Besides, I'm too old for that."

"Not me," I said.

"Enough." Mother smacked a fist on the table. And though she was a short woman and even at eleven I was taller than her, I bowed my head. "You heard what your father said. Günter, you'll help with laundry. Hans, you'll do the ovens. I also need someone to clean the hallway stairs and sweep the sidewalk." I tuned out.

Life was going to be one big chore.

www.ingramcontent.com/pod-product-compliance
Lightning Source LLC
LaVergne TN
LVHW011004200726
843509LV00011B/986